Elevated

An Anthology of Short Stories

by

Mel Vil

First published in Switzerland in 2013 by E. M. Crisp

villemel.com

ISBN: 9782954512549

Fuck doing things the normal way.

Table of Contents

Introduction

This collection of short stories presents a range of different styles. Some may fall into the traditional category, while others are somewhat more experimental, but I hope that you will find something of value in each one.

The short-story format is one that is often overlooked, but nonetheless essential in the development of creative writing. It embodies the ideas of relevancy to plot and concision in description. There is also a lot to be learned in the use and deployment of time frames.

I aim to challenge some traditional ideas of writing fiction. To do this I have tried to combine elements of poetry and prose with those of the plastic and cinematographic arts. What modern art museums show us time and time again is that the form of works has morphed consistently. This began to creep into literature during the middle of the last century, but has since vanished.

Where I have taken a separate path from the silver-screen, however, is in the use of shuffled time frames. Whilst I appreciate how this has been adopted to meet the ever-shifting attention spans of the modern audience, I prefer to maintain shorter story arcs and assume a linear path. *One last thought* and *Bullet points* are the two exceptions to this rule, but with the latter, the path is linear, yet fragmented in such a way as to reflect the trauma caused by terrorist attacks.

No art form prevails over the other. One may wander down an untrodden path, but all must advance together. Modern art challenges the audience's expectations.

And so the modern short story must do so too. I hope that in this selection of stories, you will be able to conceptualize for yourself the extent to which this is possible.

Enjoy the stories and please share them!

EMC

Snakebite and pitfall

Biting hindsight has exaggerated my mental reconstruction of the period we spent in chains together. As a refugee, he told the fate of his departed lands and people. As a weaver, he spun riddle, not sermon, thick with morality, leaving me in angry contemplation. As a prophet, he was the initiative I needed to realise independence from my reality, eventually breaking a suspicious addiction that had, for so long, had my perception comically cheated.

The preface was abomination and abhorrent carnage, too gruesome to recount. As the dust settled, his people, *El Pueblo*, struggled to hide their grief, never before had they experienced such evil. Following mourning, *El Pueblo* stood back up demanding action from their leader, *El Rey*. Swift, decisive and immediate action, to remove the threat of further pain and avenge those lost.

In response to his subjects' cry, *El Rey* stood before them, patriotically announcing "I will, my beautiful people, without fail or delay, stand up to and defeat he who dares such insurgent manoeuvres on our lands; our sacred and blessed lands. Surely, he must be ignorant of our love of life and expectation to live without such outrage." With this, *El Pueblo*, happy in the security of their leader's solid and proven word, turned back to reality but were only welcomed by a semi-normality, as even these fresh words in their ears could not drown loss resounding loudly in their hearts.

El Rey turned to his counsel, "Most learned advisers, I seek your wisdom… for I see not *El Enemigo*, just his footprint in our hearts and cities." His advisers shook their heads, for their master, despite strength of body and will, had not the quickest intellect. They explained to him how those responsible for the attacks although long gone had left behind a parasite. This was *El Enemigo*, the legacy that now plagued *El Pueblo*'s minds.

Their explanation calmed *El Rey*, but he remained doubtful and with many questions. How can he exist only in the minds of men? How can he be invulnerable to violence and weapons? How can I show my people a faceless enemy? I will not deceive them!

Their solution, indeed deceitful, fated to become a Trojan Horse for their own gates, was to destroy an embodiment of *El Enemigo*. It appeared, however, both logical and virtuous to *El Rey*, who then sought his two closest allies seeking both support and supporter.

Passionate welcome and fraternity accompanied talk of that passed and that to come. Similar convictions were shared, "I see no other way, your counsel are indeed wise, the people themselves must deny the existence of this enemy, or we hand them the responsibility," commented one. He went on to describe a potential candidate for the role of *El Enemigo*, "… of simple background, neither rich nor powerful… of evil mind and persuasive charm… unpredictably destructive… the analogy of worsening outlook." They agreed on action and left, strong in their bond, each for their homelands to publicise the angry culprit of their vexation.

Woefully *El Rey* discovered on his return that defending a conceptual foe had practical problems. During his absence his people had been weakened and their antagonist seethed between dwellings and secreted from places of work. Knowing the importance his countenance bore, *El Rey* cast aside his disappointment, drew back his shoulders, inhaled deeply and announced, "My People! Good news!"

The cover story, as it was, played well with the common man. Although not understanding fully how this distant and humble figure was the cause of his vexation, he endeavoured to return to normal life, ignorant of his deception. And so he worked, ardently, to support his armies sent to destroy *El Enemigo*.

It was not long before *El Rey*'s generals reported sufficient destruction their target's capacity, but he, shamefully, had escaped. News of this certain success had not the predicted effect, causing *El Rey* to turn again to his oracles. Shaking their heads in their accustomed fashion they explained that his choice of effigy was not appropriate, advising to select someone more conspicuous.

He became more troubled. His counsel had reminded him of the consequences of another failure, of losing *El Pueblo* were they to feel obliged to act themselves. His allies, however, were becoming impatient, they met again, electing this time a more dangerous and destructive character, one more readily recognisable, and set immediately to his destruction and the overthrow of his distant empire. The situation spiralled out of control; with defence forces abroad battling counterfeit rivals, *El Enemigo* effortlessly ventured farther onto *El Rey*'s shores. Saturated by this infectious parasite and without hope, invented successes no longer held weight; neither victory overseas nor victorious speeches soothed *El Pueblo*. Distracted on both sides *El Rey*, however, refused to give up his prospect. Despite seeing the sojourn grow indefinite, he scrabbled furiously to invent new light in his long, dark and never-ending struggle. Each time without success.

My partner in chains, one of few to escape, had left status quo, his people defiled and with no faith left in their leader. Contemplating this abysmal situation my companion added an apt analogy, *"no hay que tocarle los huevos al perro para ver si tiene dientes filosos, ya sabemos...* why touch the dog's balls, we know he has sharp teeth."

In this moment I didn't realise we were refugees from the same land having been away for so long myself. I did realise, as you too will have probably guessed by now, *El enemigo* was a guise for Fear, a malignant parasite incapable of committing its own atrocity. Instead, it walked in the shadows and like a shyster impeded the reparation of scars of both mind and soul. Disgusted but resolved into taking action I made my escape from chains, intent not only on finding him but also ridding the world of his presence; fake cowardly villain that he is.

A good number of years passed after that day of decision. To all four proverbial corners of the globe I travelled in search of him, especially wherever Danger lurked, for I knew them to be accomplices. Asia bore my first witnesses. Having struck casual conversation on a train through India we inevitably conversed on the high risk of travel on that mode of transport. I questioned their insistence to which a fellow passenger smiled politely and explained there were neither alternatives nor choice. "The men of this train will all tell you the same, but among them you won't find Fear."

In the Himalayas I encountered foreigners intent upon scaling the extreme peaks. Surely, I thought, they must fear that which can so easily go askew on the mountainside: avalanche, mountain sickness, ice bridges collapsing… "No," they would reply between laughs, "you must understand the frustration and agitation we've felt since first tempted to climb to the roof of the world." They could not let opportunity slip them by, sat at home, to them that was the epitome of fear. Their countenances, as their replies, betrayed nothing, "All we fear is Fear himself, the one you seek, but you won't find him following us."

The Americas multiplied the worst of what Asia had had to offer. Between towering mountain and precipitous valley again I found travel mildly preoccupying. Roads barely etched into the rocky sides of the Andean plains were unforgiving of the slightest mistake and struggled to support their passengers. A plethora of white crosses by the wayside indicated clearly to those who rely on these roads that they belonged to Death. Fear had no place to set ambush here.

Ignoring the high risk of partisan attacks I ventured remote mountain and jungle; regions unwelcoming to native and stranger alike. But instead of uprising, violence and hatred in the common man's heart, I found warm embrace, serene love and higher concern for my safety than his. "Here you will not find Fear," he would tell me, "to be afraid or not is one of the few choices they cannot make for us. Life must go on."

It appeared Fear was on the run, perhaps not from me but from the underdog's stronger will. Africa, I was sure, held neither sufficient strength nor chance to expel Fear; Disease and Pestilence would bear him good host. Although this continent of religiously-proportioned hazards struggled still with the dearth of food and water, I found short-fallings in education were becoming just as deadly.

Even in Africa's white heart, hinterland more accommodating of basic sustenance, where War reigns, Fear was not welcome. I asked his whereabouts of soldiers, only to hear how the savagery perpetrated by their enemies would make even Fear, the hardiest of stomachs, change face and leave. "I will die," one teenage soldier told me, "in a manner far beyond your worst imagination. If I am lucky will it be a death more honourable than many of those I've already seen." He reminded me of a proverb originating not so far away, 'to die bravely in battle carries more honour than to die cowardly in a tent,' although I saw nothing honourable in dying slowly, in spasms, in the middle of the street, at fourteen-years old. Here too, Fear had fled a horrible Death.

Remorselessly I continued. Visiting the terminally ill I saw Death's sermons on life and its inevitable and unrelenting circularity had fallen on kind ears. With monks, shaman and other holy men I received repeatedly the same answer, "Fear," they would recite, "is perhaps more powerful, but love is longer lasting." Until one day, wandering musingly through an Oceanic outback, I found my luck had changed. A recently-qualified snake catcher told me how he had since expelled Fear, "there… under that tree you'll find the one you seek, I left him there myself just a few moments ago."

But under his tree, solitary against infinity, I found not a soul. I rested wearily against the trunk. From the branches a snake watched me, "Relax," he said as I caught his eye, "I mean you no harm. Tell me, who do you seek so far from home?"

I told him of the cowardly foe, one who eluded me at every turn and how the snake catcher had left him here, beneath the tree, but that all I found was the snake himself. He dropped to the ground.

"But by what name does he escape you?" Upon hearing my answer he looked at me knowingly then blinked but before his eyes had reopened he had sprung forward and buried his fangs into my leg. Venom and blood mixed, neither hope nor faith endorsed my struggle. Releasing his teeth he spoke thus, "I apologise for my lies. I cannot apologise, however, for my venom, it is deadly and knows no other way."

His charming lisp soothed me in this brief moment. "Relax, Death hasn't found you yet." I questioned then the purpose in his bite. "At times we search for ideas so foreign we expect them to reside abroad; at other times, for things so long-lost, we find it absurd looking for them where they were left. You mistakenly perceive the object of your quest as being too large to reside within yourself. It is not a looking-glass that you lack. You blind yourself with an overgrown ego. This is the purpose of my poison. This is what it will kill." And there he left me, under his tree, contemplating my wounds and a long overdue journey home.

In the days and weeks since my return and with my renewed insight I immediately found fear, here, in our modernised society, in houses and buildings where we live and work and in the conscious mind of man and woman. Here, where the dangers we preoccupy ourselves with everyday are both imaginary and uncertain, manufactured by profiteers boundlessly investing lives in their little reality. We don't spend time distressing dogs to see how sharp their teeth are, so why do we create things in our lives to lose and fear? It is unnecessary but not inconsequential, turning a potential friend into an angry fearless danger. So why, when

we have nothing to lose and nothing to fear, do we fear
losing everything and letting sleeping dogs lie?

One last thought

It's funny how some things slip your mind so easily, I'd forgotten until now I'd been a child once. But now it is as clear and real as the outcome of the next few spilt seconds. As if I were them I can see myself from my parents perspective leaning over my pram to tickle me, strange though… to see myself from their eyes.

But my earliest memory, a visit to a duck pond, is a memory that's always stuck with me, a clear set of still images interspersed with blankness, the ducks, the trees, the water, everything except me in fact. But I know how I would have looked, the red jacket, so new it was a few sizes too large, brand new and still as red as valentines. I have red boots too, shiny and always wet with something. Navy blue shorts and paper-white legs add to the contrast. There's a photograph of me dressed like this, that's why I remember it now, it must have been in the park, I'd these big red cheeks, bloated and round like I was hiding apples inside.

That picture was taken in autumn, the leaves toasted golden caramels and spread across the green grass like a pile of jigsaw pieces. There are even leaves red enough to complement my cheeks, jacket and boots. We play in the leaves in the park, Antoine and I, building piles as tall as we were then run through them kicking and laughing. Autumn was the best time for best friends, but we grew up, I remember photograph after photograph of me growing up, the one that is clearest to me now is from when I was 9 or 10 years old.

The first memory of not being a child any longer, my cheeks receded, this particular photograph went on the sideboard in the living room, my parents pride and joy, it has never moved. If we went there right now, me and you, it'd still be there. I can see so many more photographs in my football uniform, another autumn memory. I loved football, loved it like you love reading and I loved autumn, but not like I loved the spring.

Spring was the turning point, it was the indicator of the holidays. Spring nights and daydreams spent filling myself with anticipation and plans of the hobby into which I engage my idle summer forces. One summer my father and I built kites, ready for the autumn and her strong winds. We built an army of them. I can remember flying the ones we liked best in the warm dry winds of October, we even named the biggest kite October Win's. But it was making of the kites and enjoy most, by the time we were flying them my loose attention is dreaming of football once more.

Every year, in autumn, my father and I make our pilgrimage to the same old tailor to have my new football jersey embroidered with my school's coat of arms and my dad's old shirt number on the reverse. The old man was my grandfather in the absence of a real one, every year we visit him and every year he greets me with the same smile and the same 'my how you've grown,' the chalk sometimes falling from behind his ear when he smiles too widely. He smiles more than the memories of my grandmother, she was stern and too strict but it still doesn't stop me from presenting her with a tear on my cheek at her funeral.

At that age I didn't cry much, instead I rebel in a teenage fashion. There are few photographs from that period. Antoine and I would play truant on those days at school, hiding in an alley until we were sure the bus had passed. Then we'd take our acne-plagued but innocent faces home, where we could spend the rest of the day inventing new games in the house and pretending we knew how to cook in the kitchen.

The memories of playing children fade fast as those of exams invade, the government too crowded our horizons with frowning faces one day, sending us to the sick bay to be stared, prodded and picked at. The stare is so hard, they look like somebody has rubbed their colour out. I'd only been to the sick bay once before then, once after a fight with a monster called Bill. My mother has come to take me home that day, she is friends with the nurse, so we had met before, they smiled at each other and look sympathetically at my swollen eye and bloodied nose. I'm glad they smile.

But our childhoods had always been filled with friendly and familiar faces, until this day, the day they push me, lonely, into the sickbay with this woman, this new monster and this new sickbay, cold and inhospitable. Her white face broadcasts her intelligence and lack of adventure, but it sags through the years of disappointment, reaching down and blending seamlessly into her starchy white collar. Her heavy wool suit too is not of the fond reds, greens or yellows of my autumn memories, but more like a child's experiment, the kind where you try to invent a new colour by combining the whole palette, but only ending up with nothing, a putrid slur of visual disquietude.

– SO?!?!?, she doesn't speak she announces, what do YOU want to be?!?!?! I grew up that afternoon.

The memories from here on in are of study and perseverance, exams and textbooks, cold showers and cooked breakfasts. The discipline helped my complexion and with the inevitable but tearful move from home, I was liberated. From school to university was a step forward from being less than nobody. Suddenly, I was somebody. Far from friends and family, but happy, no longer the child's lifestyle, the space allowed me an enjoyable transition to adulthood. My progress astounds even me, the long nights of loneliness never came to bearing, instead I excel in all I start. Football, studying and even with the fairer sex. I work effortlessly to the top of my class and even win an engineering prize in my first year. The trophy I give to my parents as a way of saying thank you, they cry for me and place it next to the photo I told you about, then later when I receive my degree they place a photo on the other side of the trophy, the three of us together at my graduation.

I play the last match of the season the next day, destined to be my last match. At least I am going out with glory, scoring the winning goal in injury time. The entire team are running towards me, they are going to knock me unconscious when they all land on my yellow clad chest. A painful but memorable image, they are all crowded over me as I wake up, muddy grins and matching jerseys. Now though, as if this day was the last in which colour was a legal substance, the world took a different hue, the smiles became lips and the bright eyes dark sagging and folded skin.

The grown up world, chanting monotonous corporate slogans and slow marching to the drum beats of appraisal meetings and review boards, brought me nothing but serious faces. Interview panels lined us up and investigated us as if we were livestock. This motionless inspection turns into my first boss, his Monday morning greyness and his grey-green shirts and suits of only slightly varying shades of the same colour. His colourless ties point to his bulging eyes and piggy glasses, sweet and innocent but the antitheses of having fun.

Ten years slide by like pyramid bound stones on their way up. I can see only a few memories as I slogged away at my first engine, its birth-cycle slides by now like butter skiing the virgin slopes of new potatoes. The first presentable draft, the first scale model, the prototype, shiny and purring. Six years from conception to production the first one is coming off the line now, six years of gruelling in such appalling state of recollection. Leaving me here with my boss and factory floor boys, faces as grimy and matt as the dried concrete oil slick on which we stand. We break a bottle of champagne over the manifold and a few solitary flash bulbs extinguish their lives in sorry record of this event. The four years that follow, do so with similar states of high inertia. But were interrupted.

Dissolved as I was in my work I'd no idea of what was going on in the outside world. Then I suppose none of us did. But I sit now staring at my Monday morning attempt to perfect the fuel delivery system, listening first to the offices fall silent then to the sound of war breaking out on the radio. I guess you might have seen it coming, well, we didn't. The greyest part of my life has just had its canvas pulled from behind it, the dried cracking oils left unsupported fall to the ground. No time to say goodbye to the friends I never made or to the dream girl I never met. Now I move to the next chapter in my life, now I meet the sternest face of all, yours.

– What do you MEAN you don't know how to use explosives? And you call yourself an engineer? slamming your T-bone palms on the desk in front of me. Spoken like a true sergeant but do you expect me to be 'on the ball' two hours after having said goodbye to my parents, my career, so long and laboriously worked for and cut short in return for nothing more than your critical brow with its furrows deeper than the trenches we cower in day in day out. If only you knew how threatening you are, of course I know how to use explosives, I just never have. Half the division jumped at the familiar boom of 'why are you wasting my time?' Well, you know now I wasn't, my efforts at university remain fresh in my mind, confident in them then as I am now. But still I can feel the trembling the first time corporal Glee handed me the white waxy block, you're there, you remember? Looking over my shoulder with a cold judging smile. I can hardly hold it in my hand it unnerves me so much and all you have to say is 'how lucky I am we don't have to kill people in the 'Engineers'.' Well, I hesitate now to be insubordinate but you were wrong Sar'nt.

I can still see the matchstick men and matchbox cars as they topple from my first bridge, spinning randomly as they plummet into the steamy white froth of the valley's welcoming haven. We didn't see them hit the bottom, Tom and I, you remember Tommy don't you? He is here with me, tears running down his cheeks clearing a line of 'known ground' though the brown and green paint that hides our true colours. The image is burned to my retina, his mixture of pain and awe, but we made a pact that day to not cry anymore. And we didn't but we shed more lives instead, trading many lows for few highs, but we won daily in comparison to the day I kneel with his head my lap looking down at his heart pumps the last few drops of blood through the gash in his neck. Still I promised him I wouldn't cry so I don't, but I hold pain for him that is only now about to die away. But the image never will.

The years since then, however many they are, fell like

the young bodies of the men I lost during them. Fox, you wouldn't have met him, one of those who should have made it through, a winning smile and bright ginger sideburns, his full house proudly waving in my face, not the truest preface to his chest exploding leaving a ragged and bloody hole in the aces of spades and my eyes stinging with his blood. I haven't had chance to bury many so we give him a soldier's funeral, the ace tucked in his hand, it never having moved. That wasn't so long ago, months most likely, moving with unknown rhythm, some days pass like I read playboy and others like you study Sun-Tzu. Browsingly or contemplatively the nights no longer bid me asleep nor to have say on their tempo. Regardless of my unavailability to the torrid concoctions of war dreams the sleepless nights brought me instead hallucinogenic phantoms, but familiar faces like in my vision now plaguing my conscious purpose.

I was there the day they marched through the capital y'know. It's clear as day; they parade in rank and file through parliament square. I'm crouched alone in a recess in some half-started half-finished and half destroyed building, my only visual stimulus the gut wrenching sight through the hole in the plaster and dust of the wall. My stomach rebels more at the sight of the switchbox in my hand. It calls me like a postcard from a friend long lost. I can't look at it, and I refuse to, as I hit the switch. I can't look at it, not even now, nor at the aftermath of its destruction. But can my mind's delineation be worse than any reality, aptly storing a home video of their victorious procession and the expense of its young lives. This must be by a furlong the lowest point there is, no bridge, no building tank or object attaches my explosive to these soldiers. I have killed. Killed with no justification or vindication, without and by long lacking excuse, I guess now we both know how it feels to be violated.

And now look at us, now, look at what we are: scavengers, ducking in and out of the bloody mist of desert trenches making little ground for large loss. We're not a nation any more, we're guerrillas, we wear the same beard, the same torn uniform and see through the same glazed eyes. But you, you've lost that stern look, you look like a rabbit caught in life's headlights. Your rusty shaving mirror, still the same one? Stopped any bullets yet? At least you can manage a laugh, not me. We know the reality of death now too, a recent victim grey faced and blue lipped by our side, his eyes weep a different colour to yours. That's it y'know, my last memory, I wish there were more, but I can feel again now the wrenching in my stomach as you tell me you had to kill this kid yourself as his screams of agony were giving away your position, I wonder if reality will be my last memory, I wonder if I will remember this bullet stopped in mid-air boasting in slow motion in front of me, begging for permission to penetrate my throat, its callous spin and dire consequence mock my life, like the bad last card at a crooked blackjack table it creeps innocently toward me unaware of its de-liverer's bad intention.

Four play sex by numbers

One takes home some sexy winnings from the casino, Two and Three too. Two and Three have a sexy ease about them. One is in the mood for celebrating both the odds and the winnings, and they both fit the party in mind. Giggles and smiles accompany the journey but One's mind slips to Four. The light filled trips nears One's apartment; the *soirée* is developing in each in mind. Four is dancing in One's head, completing the four figure fantasy. They would be four, if Four is willing to imbibe something alcoholic and then perhaps something even more intoxicating. Living close by, Four is a small deviation. With an index finger, One caresses the building's entry phone, heart pounding like first love. Four is having a quiet night alone. The sexy voice oozes from the box. 20 minutes however would allow anticipation to fill the pipeline and give opportunity for Four to 'get pretty'. Two and Three are well into the swing and miss this gist.

With Four soon to be *en route*, One, Two and Three arrive. All undress socially, sprawling mind, body and garment alike on the long, low and sleek sofas. One pops some champers, gliding around the grand room smiling suggestively. Two and Three smile back, but are no longer smiling at each other, something drags between them. Whatever weighs on their smiles fails on their pulses. Their hearts rage as they eye One placing exotic eats and tropical treats on the glass sheet below their bare elevated feet. Swirling and swishing, One's opens a single shirt button with each addition to the ambience. Surrounded by the cosmopolitan greens of the decor, the blazing colour of One's shirt is more representative of the colour pumping through each wrist and temple. The next enticement is the spicy tang from the speakers, drums and jeers bounce out from every corner of the velvet clad chamber.

They call a toast to champagne and winning. Eye contact, needless to say, is full. The tempo surges past flamboyant, suggestive of hot nights with sexy people in Caribbean rooms and condensation wallpaper. The mental undressing and chinking of sleek and weightless crystal glasses is interrupted by the chime of the door, Four. One's devoted heart saunters to its calling. The heat escaping from the gaping *chemise* condenses droplet by droplet side of the celestial glass. With angel in hand, One dances in harmony with the purity of inside. One devotedly focuses the same index finger, this time seducing the image on the video entry screen. Reaching for the key button Four's path is unlocked. One makes further excuses and slides down the stairs to greet Four privately. There they can flirt in seclusion, lifting Four to the speed of the night.

Two and Three take opportunity from the champagne groove to settle differences. Coldly staring into each others' eyes. Only for a split second, the duration of a single skip of desire, is there any fluctuation in the temperature otherwise unknown even in the deepest corners of space. Underneath lust boils, in the form of imprisoned liquid hatred. They stand off like angry slobs in traffic blocks.

One's tempting lyrical caresses append Four's pre-arrival heat with their own sinful creations. Less than moral wooing pauses as Four feels the heat rising down the stairs. Two and Three await Four, yearning to feel warmth again. The tempo of the temperature flux and music multiply as the numbers double. Racing hearts and pulses forgo the need for introduction. Four party people, four pretty faces. The only deficiency is one glass angel. One responds, retiring to fetch a glass from heaven that will allow four to drink in harmony the fruits of the land. Four sits, knees together to one side, presence protected by a solitary hand. Heart drumming and cheeks singing to the radiant vibe. The cold freshness from whence Four came dissipates from the fresh skin but Two and Three see new opportunity for their glacier freezing stares. Four misunderstands the icy-coldness for flirting and giggles shyly at envy mistaken for lust. Regret still freshly sewn is unfelt allowing good feelings to the forefront.

One flourishes back onto the scene, fresh glass freshly filled. Smiling at Four their eyes meet, sewing a different seed in each different body. One's touch restores Four's grace and glide and slides the gentle frame back to its supple leather perch like ice on summer skin. Handing Four a look of lust and a glass of infinitely unknown bubbles, One's attention diverts back to Two and Three. Collapsing between them in a moment's escape from the passion fruit of the eye, arms around them and smiling through closed eyes. One's bubble filled head drops back to look at the ceiling, vacuuming sexual confrontation into each lung via flared nostrils. In this position One revels in the uncontrollability of body and mind when life is at full pace. The moment hypnotises with teasing temptation and infinite outcomes. At an imaginary crossroads, the devil offers his soul in exchange for a moment in One's body, but right then the rhythm of the samba falls in line with One's pulse, throwing both back into their respective fires.

Particles of oxygen, energised by the tension and fear-ing their safety, flee for refuge in the corners of the room, watching over the scene from afar. They see the deadlock across the chest of One, Four, sipping champagne timidly looking mainly to the floor. The situation's explosiveness requires a few things more: between Two and Three an ice-pick, between them and Four the opposite, armour plating. Between them and One a clear explanation, perhaps accompanied with a drawing of an apology. Between the last pair, One and Four, the most subtle item remains unrealised, that of privacy and seclusion.

Bringing reality back to the conscious mind, One steps briefly through the raging battlefield, allowing the devil a brief look at Four. Captured by the split-second of evil, a predisposition to suggestiveness grips Four by a sensitive organ deep inside, somewhere else, further than the mind's first thought, way beyond, where frenzy burns and a fuse shortens, threatening to disrupt the forces that hold the darker side at bay.

One word who listens

Primo,

This letter is going to sound a bit strange. I have just had some bad news over the telephone. I can't explain it to you easily as we haven't seen each other for such a long time, so I am going to tell you the entire story. How long has it been, a year? Well, since then my life has been a little out of touch or perhaps life a little out of touch with me.

Quite a while ago, I started getting this strange sensation when I called people, you know, on the phone. It's difficult to describe how but it felt as if the person I was calling wasn't listening and that somebody else was. At first I felt a bit paranoid, but believe me, I am not, and I know why now. I don't want to tell you straight away as its going to be hard for you to take too, but it'll become clear so don't think I am some kind of mad lunatic if you can read this.

Anyway, back then, I was sure somebody was listening to, or worse, recording my conversations. I called the telephone company but I don't think they really listened to me either, one of them even hung up on me as if I was some lonely and bored housebound kid. It felt silly then, being ignored as if I was still a kid. You know me, you know I'm not the type to pay a lot of attention to what's going on in the world, unless it affects me, and that's how I felt.

So, there I was, alone and too scared to use the phone. It occurred to me that the one who listens may have been doing so all the time. This thought wouldn't leave me alone. It called me to listen to the phone. It had my brain convinced that the sound of my not talking was making the one who listens want me to talk more.

It scared me. I stopped making calls, not being able to bear any longer that quiet bit before the dial tone and those cold damp breaths as I dialled, the creepy echoes of all that was spoken on the line. I did try, honestly, to continue my normal life and in doing so let the phone ring as it always had, attending the calls of my mother and my friends.

I tried to listen to them, but all I could hear was the background noise. Their daily lives went in one ear and out the other, as I searched for some clue as to who was listening. I would interrogate Mum about what she was doing in the house, hoping it might be some kitchen utensil that was causing the whirring even though I feared it was a tape recorder. Or if it was father snoring or worse the devil laughing. Naturally, they didn't answer my silly questions.

My friends, you know, are less domesticated but still the noises were ever-present, and still they seemed to not hear me when I talked with them. It was a pain to talk with them all, those noises, small as they were, I swear to you, each and every one has given me a grey hair.

Then, I began to alienate my friends, I guess my behaviour changed, maybe I did become paranoid. Not without good reason, with some devil hounding you it's difficult just to carry on. The sound of the phone ringing would send me storming through the house closing window, curtain and door to drown the street noise, stopping all clocks and turning off all the electrical things. Then I would move away from all the wires to reduce interference. I knew the silent breaths and placid heart beats were not mine.

I would sit quietly nodding and shaking my head to my family and friend's questions, so as not to disturb the silence I could gather in my head. Every little crackle in the line sent jerks simultaneously through random muscles in my cold wet shivering body. Every time they would reach a climatic point of a story I would listen more closely waiting for the one who listens to make some mistake. A laugh or shyness in an erred response. I needed some explanation.

Then came the cold, long winter nights, bringing me further down, then my normal behaviours disappeared. It sounds like pathetic behaviour, but I would press my shivering body against the inner-most wall of the house, solitary in its quietest corner with the phone in my lap. Listening over and over to the dial tone and to find out what was behind it, to find the secrets of the one who listens. I would listen until that higher pitch began, the one that warns you the receiver is off. That dreadful noise signified nothing to my sensitised ears, so I managed, for a few blissful days, to let it go. But then the thought struck, like the pinch of regret. What of the noise beyond that higher pitch. What comes next?

So I sat, the reverberating sound of that second tone penetrating deep into my already weakened soul, never-ending. I couldn't bear to listen long enough, until a few nights ago that is, I fell sound asleep. Then that strange thing happened, you know when you're sleeping peacefully with music on, but if someone turns it off you wake up? That's what happened. When that second tone stopped I woke, like a shot. I picked the ear-piece from my lap where it had fallen, my heart pounded as it reached my ear. And what did I hear?

The sound I heard was that one you hate so much, the one we came all the way to the city to escape. Not some new concoction of those stupid telephone companies but an irritating and uninventive sound. Worse than perpetual screams, it sounded over and over, a sound that makes you cover you ears and beg for it to stop. Over and over, incessantly mocking my obsessive addiction it preyed upon my fears that sickly familiar sound of silence.

But it was false pretence. The line wasn't dead, my highly tuned ears readjusted. Then, I could hear the voices as they chattered, I could hear the infinite voices. The noise of a million exterminated lives, the combined garble, the sound of every voice ever born living or dead sounding at once. The choir of baritones and altos, angels aloft and fallen, the voice of us, me and you and every other born without the gift of song, the voice of the one who listens, even the voice of the voiceless could be heard, mixed into this silent cacophony of chaos.

My soul quietly and slowly filled with the random deranged screaming that can only have been composed inside the walls of hell. It emerged into a muddy drone, as silent as gas creeping out of deadly cracks in the pipes and filling our homes. As frightening as the sound of ice cracking under cold water multiplied a thousand times. It had me. The choir of pandemonium had me transfixed.

Day after day, quiet and solitary, I listened and deciphered. It gets worse. I don't want to write any more, even if you can read this letter you're going to think it is the product of some delusional prankster, but anyway, I must finish. Last night some evil part of my brain decided the next step would be to question the one who listens. Stupidity, perhaps, but once sewn this thought took no time to take control of my lips. But the broken word was hardly created in my head before my ear was disturbed.

I can't explain the disturbance I caused in hell with a simple and unpronounced word. The noise surged into my ear diving straight down towards my heart where it crushed the blood in its chambers turning to into a molten charge of rage, a rage that tested the vessels of my enfeebled brain. The seething heat burned my flesh from within and evaporated the air in my lungs. I felt like I hadn't breathed in a year. It was so confusing, I thought for a while I had gone deaf, blood appearing from my ear. Ironically the blood was just from my obsessive listening.

Over a few minutes I calmed down, my heart slowed and my ability to hear returned, but when it did, I was left again with the same dreadful nothingness, silence, real silence this time. And real silence was not what I wanted to hear, I wanted to hear something to prove that I was still in the land of the living. My heart pounded, striking like a muffled bell, my fear pounding entrance at the doors of my soul. Nothing. I spoke again, I heard the voices retreat, seemingly in synthesis of answer, their cowardly motion screamed like a scorned cat.

The quiet was soon disturbed. They gave me their answer. This time my ears held the noise, the noise of every one of those infinite voices screaming in unison, a noise I hope you will never have to hear. A sound perfectly indescribable in mortal words. I thought about the sound, it was like the heaven and hell colliding, like gods striking sword blows, like every cloud in the sky slamming into the ocean.

It was a sound that shook my soul and surely loosened the foundations of hell from where it must have come. How can I describe its evil to you, it was like the articulation of every lost soul from our sickened history crying its pain to sleep.

I swear to you that my heart stopped, frozen clean on the brink of the fatal beat that would have made it implode. Like a feather hitting the ground after falling from the sky, it rested, cold, in perfect stasis, to be forever lodged on the brink of moving once more. My weakened body was crushed, only the reverberating shivers of my muscles shifted the half-frozen blood around my body. My skin was parched dry like it had been exposed to those same fires of hell. I wished to beg the voices calm but my vocal cords had suffered the same fate as my heart.

The voice repeated like a cold echo. My life seemed to remain, although as if it was in some frieze, on hold until the noise had stopped. I trained my ear to its torturous scream soon discovering it was repeating one word over and over, it was a bitter-sweet shock that such noise, like metal edges torturing flesh, could produce a word that might explain what was going on in my 'life'. So, for hours, until a few minutes ago, I sat and listened, intent on deciphering the word.

And some minutes before I began to write you this letter I heard the word. Then I was able to replace the receiver. The paralysis and the fixation ended with my understanding of that one word and then I wanted nothing more than to replace the receiver.

That one word pierced my frail heart and now I know why I can't repeat it even to you, so I write to you instead…. there are tears on my page, help me, please help me…. help me get back what that one word has taken away. It has changed the course of my life for the infinite worse. A word has ended my normality, my reality. One split second of recognition led to by an obsession. One little harmless word. One word. One word. How did I not know? Why didn't you tell me? Why was I left to find out this way? I can't write it to you… but I have to, the one word from the one who listens. The word that told me what I have be-come…

welcome

Lonely old cat

He looked lonely. To a certain extent, in just a few respects, he was. In other respect, he was just waiting. He gazed from the window, feeling the city as it eased past his face, carrying its familiar bouquet of sounds and smells. He was just waiting. Waiting for the meal he was preparing and the company with whom he would share it. The meal, steamed vegetables and salmon, needed more time and less attention; Julian promised this would be the last occasion he would inspect it, did so and turned again to the open window.

He decided instead to review his day, for the view held little to be analysed, little new at least. Julian would regularly take time from his day to inspect its inner workings, clearing the bad thoughts or confrontations in hope of starting the next morning afresh. It was a kind of meditation, a coping mechanism for later life that he had developed over the long years. It had worked well for many of those years, but he was reaching a point in his life where days held little to analyse.

He turned to the evening instead, warm and dry. It eased past his face carrying those sounds and smells of the city which surged from beyond his visual range. Directly he could see little but blackness, silhouetted roofs and walls rear-lit by the orange-yellow hum of the city. The monotony of the straight lines broken only at random intervals by the occasional tree, snippets of neon lights misspelling words in the blackness. His city lived. Like clockwork, it ticked and it never missed a stroke.

His thoughts were interrupted by the most awful of

screams. A cat, he thought. The screams, indeed those of a cat, halted Julian's train of thought. His attention had been captured by their horrific nature, neither varying in pitch nor tone yet beginning to repeat at seemingly random intervals.

The cat, he thought, is stuck somewhere. No other source or predicament could cause such anguish in such a proud animal. The cat, he thought, is stuck somewhere and nobody is going to help it. He looked back at the pots on the stove but resisted the temptation to lift their lids and turned back to the window. The screaming continued. The cat, he thought, is stuck somewhere, injured and no one is going to help it. He thought briefly of leaving to help it himself, but he was past that kind of antic at his age, even if he could find it, he probably wouldn't be able to reach or help it.

The cat, he thought, is stuck somewhere, injured and probably bleeding and no one is going to help it. The cat, one of the most self-sufficient of animals, had indeed seen its fate, realised it and opted for the loss of one of its nine social lives as the cost of a real one. Back on the stove, the pots remained happy with their lack of attention, frustrated Julian went back to the sounds of the city. The cat, he thought, is stuck somewhere, bleeding, no one is going to help it and it having realised this fact has given in to the last option, the cry for help.

The cat, he thought, knows only to survive. Just like us. But only the cat knows what it has done or has yet to achieve, what it has and has not and whether it is a fair trade, losing face instead dying of a peaceful death. Only the cat, he thought, knows whether it's worth fighting. He wondered then, if it was natural to fight so hard, so close to the end. The noise began to sicken him, but the pots still bade him no source of escape, and so he turned to his watch for relief.

Susanne wasn't due for another twenty minutes. He was glad she was coming. Eating alone was painful enough, what if he caught a fish bone in his throat! He would have to scream like the cat, only silently and to an even less responsive audience. He shook the thought from his head, but the pots remained happy.

He decided to practice her entrance. He would show her the desire he holds for her, how he would display the desire he holds for her to stay, to stay the night and to stay longer. He would display the longing for her as a later-life partner. But not his neediness. He wouldn't scream like the cat, the poor cat, it needed help, no living animal screams with such anguish unless they are desperate, even the most demanding actor can't summon that pain from everyday-life's dull script.

Julian thought himself lucky to have his throat clear of fish bones. He still had time in which he could purr. He didn't feel the need to act desperately. No, he was filled with warm feelings upon the thought of his guest arriving and turned confidently to the window. The warm air of the city eased passed his face carrying its familiar bouquet of sounds and smells. But something had changed. Something was missing now. The screaming had stopped, and, feeling the cat's fate pass though his soul, he succumbed to the cold sensation consuming his own.

The future of inside

Unconditioned sounds reflex through the walls of my mind. Surfing through the infinite stories of information piled against its walls, the resonance of yesterday and its moments ring true, elicited by the quiet sounds of a music box. A tear drop grows, not destined for the cheek but to fill the empty chamber of a still beating heart. If I stop thinking in sounds and pictures that draw me back to yesterday, the feelings I left behind, I could discover what kind of person am I.

I forget to tell my parents that the secret to life was there all along and that my gestation was just a refractory period allowing me to gather baseline data. One's own history gathers in one hemisphere, have mankind's future is already present in the other. The process of life: transferring data from one side of the brain to the other, my memory closet. The dark side becomes reality becomes history.

Stretching the limits of inter hemispherical communication, the mind presents and image which in turn forces me to contemplate, teasing my sense of logical continuation. Surface currents stir the muscles of my face, reflective not of what drives underneath, but of the impression I want to give of that which thrives beneath. An increase in volume, a change of heart, the rhythm calling my name like smoke signals in the clouds.

Indifferential to the patterns of habit, I raise my smile and decide to join the game, I walk out of my social coma onto the *cancha[1]*. Here we are ladies and gentle-

---

[1] The football field [read: performance arena]

man. The first day in the middle of this man's life.

Day one, I get up, perhaps today might be more enlightened. The thoughts circulate my mind, in black and white, black like the night I have awoken from, white like my morning tea. I add sugar, loaf to my duties, my social restrictions. Today the rhythm has me spinning out of motor control. The words come out wrong, the lines go in the wrong place. I am free.

Day two, I get up, perhaps. The shock of normality removed feels like the loss of a loved body-part. An itch exists. An itch that will remind me of the loss of routine and habit over the coming days. Today, however, my tea is less sugary. What will be next? The change.

Increases in the temperature of my brain's core cause great pain. It spreads and my muscles turn green and acidic. They are revolting. Rebellion is felt, mutiny amongst my neurones. Time to take a break. Time to figure out what I was doing wrong.

I may see hope, but there is none in my eyes. Blinded internally by bad blood. To lose the world around me would be a relief to my senses. But to be blinded inside is like being lost in a crowd. I can no longer see what I am feeling inside. I am no longer inside my own body.

I take time to imagine how the social creature combs his hair in the mirror, dresses like he sees in glossy shoots and films, talks like his friends and heroes. He exists outside of himself. So am I now he?

The monk shaves his scalp to allow the world entrance. His appearance is nothing, words often have little meaning but invoke much interpretation. He exists inside himself. Something has changed.

I pursue the idea that one side of the human brain

holds the future, like a book, revealing the story one page turn at a time. Does a vast space, with more capacity than we can use, exist? Or are we talking fixed capacity? Like the hourglass? I dread the consequences of overflow. Am I spreading my life into the residual? The move to the future means moving to new neural areas, time bringing us nothing but keys and access codes.

The greatest steal in life is knowing the future. But I suppose the only future I have inside is my own. Although there is no harm in examining it to see who around is predictable. I calculate.

Man's weakness is in prediction. I watch him as he falls first into a repetitive cycle of lotteries and bad buys, then into the decision that he has found adulthood. But he can't understand. He stands around awaiting some pamphlet, certificate or handout. My luck is in. I have realised the stretched out brain leads somewhat further, I find the answers inside. I can refuse approaching my past, now the future shines so clearly in front of my mind's eye.

Strength is having discovered weakness. But can I forget that with no idea of direction there is no chance of getting lost. Now I have to reflexively lie about the past, invent plausible justifications and hide. All that remains is to tell my parents about a childhood that consisted of nothing but lies.

Escaping my freeze-dried habitat

I can sit and wait for waves of euphoria to wash over me like sand on the wind erodes volcanic flows lying dormant between freeze-dried mountains. But I don't think it will happen. There is more chance that I will become lost in the next thought. I have to push so hard to remain focussed in these far-away places, environments I know and in which I want to be.

It's a warm balmy night somewhere in the province. Not in the big mess but the neat and tidy tick that clings beneath its fur. The heat is intense even though it is eleven-thirty at night, probably somewhere around twenty-seven degrees. We sit and eat outside on the pavement. Watch the world go by from beer-sponsored movie-producer chairs parked at high-end garden furniture. Then take an ice cream in the same quality of chair but at a metal foldaway table.

There is a pressure that comes from inside, ordering the production of future communications. Planning how it will sound and what it will say. I role-play my own future as if it were rehearsals. And yet here I am, a man averse to practising in front of the mirror. – If you see how stupid you're going to look saying it, then that's all you be able to think about it when it's time to let it come out, so why bother?

"I am leaving you, darling", my heart starts, beating at six to the dozen, interestingly that's a close approximation to the average heartbeat of a man on his deathbed overcome by the fallen-from-grace disease formally known as old age. I find the two incompatible and start to shift in my chair.

Her eyes glaze over, and she hesitates before looking around her. She stares at me the same way she did when she walked in on her mother and I putting her senile dalmatian to sleep on the kitchen floor. I stand up and begin aimlessly walking. Reality seems like inebriation.

The world is mine

The world is mine, the echo of a thousand voices reminds me of the destiny I forge with each and every heartbeat of life. I am my experience and will become the result of my ability to learn and become wise from this. I take a ride into a symmetrical universe where what is not on the left is balanced on the right. Never the same yet encompassing. The ride is three hundred and sixty degrees.

I gather the tools I need as they lie in front of me. I must destroy this yearning to find what I had beforehand. She creation is the next path I must take. Again I have to let go of a guiding hand. Leave the past behind, having wisely extracted its only nutrient, knowledge. I'm a pimp, a hustler and a player.

Stick to recalling that which was good is living in the past. I live in the present hoping to be the future. My mindset is how I imagine the world to be in its perfect creation. My fluctuating emotional state the only interference. My negativity dampens my hopes and rain falls like a tragedy.

How will she be who he wants to be? The feeling is extraordinary and he plies his trade while at full awareness. There is no sauce, no milky tea, although one suggests these as the way forward he knows deep down that all that is necessary is already there with him. Hisself and the instrument. The emotion and the ability to record it. Taking the body away from his mind and imagining it as the extension of the computer.

The machine sits in a wry fashion on the table, its

mouth open ready to accept my diarrhoea. The projection it makes is a man in a room, wearing gentlemen's shoes with Adidas tracksuit bottoms and a bright blue jumper made of some petrochemical-based man-made fabric. There is hope. The style emerges.

It doesn't matter how he is dressed as he is out of the public eye. While he is leaving at 9.30am he is doing well. There is no need for any soul to know of his habits. The material of his mind is further yet from ever being accessible to the masses. He forces himself into secrecy yet with his ability to manage the environment he finds it difficult to not draw attention to himself.

Have compromises been taken? He takes the first sip of what he said he wouldn't touch again. New Year's resolutions become fuzzy and faint signals, weakened by the passage of the addictive substance through the darkening passages of his creativity. Justification after justification reminds him that he can never be put down, even by his own failures. His mind will always create an artificial balance, as the hall of mirrors renders him beautiful so too the flat, plate-glass reflection pounds away at his self-image. The over zealous sculptor ruins yet another unfinished piece.

Whatever is still wrong will be beaten down not only by the footsteps of the Inca runner but also the time he lacks. Always there and persistently ever-present is the indelible pacing drum, the boom of repetition that contains the rhythm of discipline. The god that is music, the slave master that is practice and persistence.

He knows the route to his goals begins with the first step yet nobody has spoken widely of steps ten, eleven and twelve; who will be the guide to his mid-life. Who will carry him over rough waters with Neptunian strides and through mountains in a Herculean demonstration of tunnelling. She is on the verge of rising from the waters with intelligence dripping from her skin.

Surface tension grips silvery bubbles which lodge between the erect blonde hairs that cover her Boudican body, follicles that have until now sustained an envelope of oxygen trapped close to her throughout this gestating metamorphosis. They peel away, no longer useful their supreme master. She calls to them from a long-boat as it draws to the edge of the lake. The conclusion is imperceptible in the shadow of her beauty; she strides from the water and onto the shore. She is produced, stands proud only to kneel, turn and lie back. She saturates the sand with her knowledge, basking her naked form in the sun. Once her skin warms and the steam finishes evaporating, she will be ready.

Back to Buenos please

Tasks and finalisations, the test of time and patience, coke and climax. The thoughts of getting a purer flow must be elevated beyond the theoretical world. Time to change the pace of this expedition. I want to lie shipwrecked and blinded with the sounds of the thumping bass as my only guide to the reality that I go along creating.

Life is always going to be full of little surprises; I have that locked down and so make my merry way with my eyes open, hands at the ready and contingencies made. There is no mistake in preparation, there is no future that can be taken away from the ready. Whatever happens I keep my *cara dura.*

The reality is simple. It presents itself. There is no need to go anywhere to try to get it. No point in trying to change it for something better. How could we change what is so heavy and laden with inertia, stop what has such momentum and dynamic features.

I strive to be on a caged walkway walking late at night over the entrance to 9th of July Avenue. Where nobody could stop me and where I would be caged in yet like a lion being tortured with a cattle prod, visible to all the world not too engrossed in driving their cars.

I want to be where my heart beats. The lure of danger illustrates an attractive painting. Pain staking pangs of hunger drive me past the all night 99c pancho stand. No time for breakfast. Thoughts of princesses kidnapped in Paraguay control my mindset. Where will the wacky weed come from if the borders are on full alert and patrol?

Time to fly to Colombia, their leaderless state lead by opposing factions needs to be brought under control. We can't have their renegades causing trouble elsewhere. Would have to take over and lead the forces down a new path, sit them all side by side. Allow them a level playing field, so they can go about hating each other as they wish.

There's not much chance of anything else happening. It's a moment in time that promotes laying the head back, maintaining eyelids stationary and eventually catching a moment of blackness. Toes warm and thoughts of the sun baking the skin dry. The pitter-patter of raindrops is really the flicker of the flame. Licks of a golden and purple ephemeral tongue.

Sharks couldn't take advantage of me with my hands tied. So what makes you think different? You sure as hell don't have that kind of bite. Take another example for instance. I have to go forwards in my progression. Your hindering attempts need not apply. I do not let them apply, take your leave and go describe the essential within.

Can we allow time to make us wait so long? I test my own patience in a half hour. There was truth in saying, there is no room for expansion, yet we take opportunity for the sake of just reward, if only we could just reward ourselves that little bit more. Nice. Time to take a bite and then the apple stops growing. My only luck is its eternally sweet nature. I know that every first bite will be sweet.

So why do we not wait for it to ripen and enjoy the entire fruit?

There comes a point where all things must be separated. Parsed, to distinguish what is my life, my dreams, my fantasy my reality and my irreality. I defy fiction in the incorporation of fact and deny fact with the direction of my pursuit. Never the less, that road is that of beauty, the destination just a car park for corpses. Once I am there my arrival will become known and announced. And that shall hopefully be the end.

I stop, therefore, thinking. The planning and precognitive strategies are merely in vain. The art is not the writing, the deciding and editing, but the doing. I must head West if I am ever to have words to sift like a prospector by the river bed. In amongst all this dirt lies the ignition of my desire. The realisation of my function and then the completion of my purpose.

The tea maker

The man walks around his house. The day after yesterday. His day's tasks have been completed. Yet it is still only the mid-afternoon. He paces, returns to his desk and reviews copies of the day's documents; the originals having already been despatched. What could he change had there been a fault? Nothing.

He considers two distinct lives. The first type of life is where he finishes the day's work and doesn't find anything changed. Nothing new. There is no radio, clock, or plate that is in any way different from the way he left it. He finishes his day's tasks and relaxes. Relaxes in an identical fashion to the previous day. Even the outside world appears the same.

He considers secondly that of change. The entire environment has been changing during the time he has been yearning nothing but stability. Why is it that he finds it hard to finish the day and relax in the feeling of accomplishment?

He can turn on 24 hour news, check messages or mails. He can look around and thank the universe for not having demolished his house, repossessed his 5.1 system, run down the battery in the kitchen clock or for not having led him to interfere with somebody else's life.

Here is a man who knows all too well how green the grass was on the other side. He begs for yesterday and has it. Like pocket fluff, however, he can't imagine how things arrived to be the way they are.

He arranges his stubby limbs on a sofa and sips through a cup of tea in less than one minute. Unconsciously. He stares at the residue, swilling it from side to side, places the cup on the low table in front and begins to stare from the window. — Tomorrow will be a new day,— he says quietly.

A cat comes sauntering through the gap in the living room door, tail erect. Gently approaching the front of the sofa she skirts along and rubs its hard and slightly sinusoidal tail on the lower side of the man's knee. He looks down. — Can't you wait until your mother gets home for attention?— he checks his watch and leaves the sofa.

In the kitchen he prepares a pot of tea, eyeing the clock repetitively. He paces and reads the backs of various food packets, comparing the nutritional values only to discard the information in favour of the clock and the pot. Pouring in the hot water and replacing the lid, he eyes the clock once more.

He places a tea cosy over the pot and lays out two cups, two saucers and a teaspoon, contemplating for a moment before beginning to slice a lemon. The cat returns and attempts to weave through the man's legs once more, causing him to push her slightly to one side. He nicks his finger on the knife's stumpy blade.

— You're a pesky little girl aren't you?— he can't help but watch the clock again. He stays transfixed by the black hands, sucking on his finger. The clock's terracotta face and black letters dwell in a dark recess high on the wall above the gap between two windows that look out to an inner-city garden. On one window, two horizontally positioned rubber suckers hold an empty bird feeder. The feeder draws the tea-maker's attention.

— Perhaps, if we started filling that bird feeder the birds would come back,— he nudges the cat with his ankle, — give you something to do.

The clock ticks to the half hour. The tea-maker is drawn to it. 4.30 pm. He pours out tea into one of the cups, adds sugar and milk. To the other cup he gently tosses in the slices of lemon, yet doesn't pour tea. — Come on, — he leans down to tickle the cat, leading her out of the kitchen and back to the sofa. The second cup and the pot of tea stay alone in the kitchen with the sounds of the terracotta clock and under the watchful eyes of the empty bird feeder.

On the sofa the man stirs the brown liquid aimlessly. With his shins pressed up against the dark teak wood of the centre table, he stares into nothing. He lays the tea-spoon in the saucer and shifts his gaze to the carpet and the fireplace.

He looks at his wrist-watch and again shakes his head. It is a slow motion that precedes his laying back in the sofa. The cat sits with its back to the French window and the city garden, it pauses from washing to look briefly at the fireplace, then resumes.

The tea-maker leaves his tea and walks through the house, opening the front door to a rush of air and sound. Traffic buzzes by on the other side of a complete row of parked cars, he stares first left then right. The street is empty of pedestrians. He returns to the sofa, sighs and begins to drain the cup of tea, again in rapid slurping, emptying the cup once more in a matter of seconds.

After letting out a pitched sigh he returns to the kitchen. He rinses both cups and leaves them to drain. He puts the milk back in the fridge, bins the slices of lemon and pours away the remaining tea. He looks over his shoulder to the terracotta clock, shakes his head and then lowers it again. He stares into the sink, resting his weight on reversed hands planted on its edge. The cat doesn't return to the kitchen.

Travel from Small Corals

Call it never land. Another place where it never rains. An exception. Today the day rain falls from the sky like life. And odours are released from their concrete and vegetable jails. Tiles and plants.

With the doors and windows open there is chance the entire house will cool down. The feeling of rejuvenation and rehydration, a stewarding wind cleans the house. With this there is energy to live another thousand days.

It's the wind, however, that best reaches the vital organs. The plants and tiles transpire and cool. They benefit. The battle between infernal heat and human physiological regulation continues. The rain will not calm puffy eyes nor dry and itchy skin. The brain's dearth of fluid has caused swelling, and its yearns for the rain to stop by as it's chased by this bully wind.

What is left to do in a country raised to hate what hated to help them grow? Filial becomes sibling and the culpability slips. Where in the world is it responsible to scream in the street: it was our fathers' faults. What is there left to do? Go home.

The end to gregariousness and affiliation. They see through. Usefulness dies. Farewells are said, as remorseful as the kin of uselessness. Finding the way in – becomes finding the way back – becomes finding the way in. Thoughts circulate yet fail to reproduce.

Return home, have troubles with the foreign subway. Escalators are reborn at the end of familiar passageways. Tunnels return original faces, situations and signs. The world from the second point of view.

Taking what used to be an old short-cut, a dead-end-faced employee tells me it is no longer a viable via. There is to have a ticket and there is to go back down the broken escalator. I turn and begin clunking down the escalator I just climbed. The descent is even further out of synch with my gait. Each step coils my lumbar and erases memories.

At the ticket window a conversation strikes off. – why do you use this stamp for the tickets? Casual comment, aimed amiably at the amiable old man.

— I worked here all my life, this used to be my job.

— And now, it is just like a hobby.

Smiling old man with his tools and rubber stamps. End of an age, start of another. The man of overlap.

Beached in conversation. The metropolitan users of the metro whirl by, lapping and ebbing, pushing me away from the main current and further into depths of the amiable old man.

— With this tool I can make a print block. Then at the end of the day slice it off and make another. — he demonstrates the wooden block and red rubber. Then adds it to the shelf rack to his side taking another.

— I have a variety, so I can be working on stamps for the following days. And well I don't know who I am kidding. I am a relic and as soon as they can afford a second machine and to train someone unskilled in how to use it I'll be swimming with these red rubber offcuts.— he dabs and casts a few red slithers off the counter into a bin somewhere below the desk.

— It's sad,— my brain replies at long last,— that your life's work should be replaced. Surely not all of these people can have places to go that are so important that they can't let other men continue to work.

— But they just throw the tickets away,— the lady operating the other ticket window jumped into the conversation between customers. — it's a ticket. It gets you from A to B. Afterwards you throw it away. Why put the effort into making something disposable. And around here all this just gets busier everyday.

I looked behind me as she offered to watch the *mêlée*. The pace and density of the crowd suggested a larger mayhem resided during the peak travel hours.

— OK, how about the travel cards. You must sell week or month passes. You could be responsible for those. Make each unique, give the customer something to think about.

— There's the biggest irony. Those are the main reason the invested in the machines. To print those travel cards.

The lady served another customer while I looked into the tired-old man's tired-old eyes. She then rotated off her seat and pulled a key chain around her neck. — You'll see why.

As she approached a wall safe on the rear wall of their office a hush went through the concourse behind me. Even as she opened the box I could feel a wave of attraction resonate through the crowd.

Producing a laminated card, the lady came over to the counter. The crowd behind were now captivated, their eyes drawn in any direction the card went. Yet it seemed like any other, albeit laminated. And so I wondered what essence it has that gave it the air of a Get Out of Jail Free card.

The crowd could no longer resist. A flurry of requests, questions and offers began. The barrage couldn't force the lady to flinch, she merely smiled at me and said, — see what you've started!

I turned around to look at what had become of my fellow citizens. Reverted to the behaviour of the *souq*. There used to be a time, and it still exists in the norm, that the underground represented the only publicly conservative area of the city life. They battered and haggled endlessly towards deaf ears before turning on each other; inspecting the goods and chattels of each other.

As I turned around to the counter I noticed the man sweeping his tools into a draw like a life-beaten miser saving crumbs. — you are like the rest of them, more interested in that than mine. Like it is some holy grail. — he paused to look me in the eyes then said, — I am sorry, I didn't mean it, but I see how the crowd excites you, you run the risk of falling into their hands. But I guess that is the future. And all because mine is only worth one journey.

— Yet you still have no idea just how few people buy this ticket that my colleague here has to fight to defend. Think of all those people in the city who can afford to travel by car or taxi. Why would they suffer the underground? Perhaps some people want to save their precious time or evade the pollution and heat. To avoid these queues in the mornings. Really I don't know. But look at the reaction of these people, they are desperate. They cannot afford to pay for all their journeys upfront.

His shoulders slumped, dragging with them further the skin under his eyes. — if only they would give this away at the beginning of the month or year and then let the passengers pay at the end.

Airplane

The centre of my world lies at my front door. I step across the threshold. Life's cold wind seemingly having ceased for the season. I can feel spring just weeks and days away.

I'd make a good risk assessor, but could never take the risks myself. We were pulled over twice in the last week, thinking we were sucking it up and holding down in San Telmo. Turns out we have only been sucking it in. Add to that these new anti-kidnap laws; PFA are rolling on whoever they want, whenever they feel like it.

I can see what is going on around me, but these poor fuckers are blind to the Good Air. I keep reminding them, mix with the locals, learn the fucking lingo, gringo. Get an idea of what is spinning on around you. One of these idiots was bothering me the other day, talking about he was so high one morning, man, when he got into the taxi, the driver said, 'where to, airplane?' His face dropped when I said *Gavión*, not *avión.*

With that cold wind no longer, the heat can rise from the gutters. And it brings the pussy with it. Less than half a block from the front door and we are surrounded by the stink. Perhaps it is warm because all these women are on heat, hanging around on street corners, as if guys would just come along and take them home.

We stop a corner and wait for some black-and-golds to pass, Jay points out four girls sitting in a corner café laughing over an eleven p.m. beer. He says 'we could take them back and fuck them, then leave again.' As if to say it wouldn't change the script.

He was just looking for a story to tell to the girls all night. Give him an excuse not to take them home, let him feel better than them. I tell him we're late and blow the girls a kiss. A joke is a joke, but there is nothing to be gained in wasting waiting opportunity by taking just any old opportunity. There is a drug and prostitute fuelled underground to be infiltrated.

It's a big dirty city, the kind in which hustlers don't stand out of the crowd. The crowd stands out. The hustlers are kept in business because the boats and planes keep coming in. As one sucker arrives he fills the space left by yet another empty-pocketed loser making his way home. Real life casino.

I strongly believe I don't belong in a place like this. My innate humanitarianism and good karma strongly clash with the emotions and behaviours that here are considered norms. I put it at the back of my mind and take another pill.

Flash to the next morning: the car park outside *Pachá*. *Pachá,* Latin-America's pink palace version of Ibiza, beached on the banks of the River Plate basin. Two drugged up girls cower inside my parka. The sun is shining but the return of the cold wind has us gripped together tightly. Typewriter-faced Rodrigo is the only crim on the block. He flits about, jabbering, clanking his jaw and tucking into a *pancho.* He twitches and rubs his oversized beanie with the back of his hand, scratching at his forehead. The dull but recognisable music stops. The usual suspects pour from the gates. Brightly clothed and bleary eyed.

Rodrigo is small time, Small Fish. I send him away with the two girls. Here comes my catch of the day. Fresh from the riverbank. Leaving the girls with

Rodrigo gives me space to operate.

The face that stands out of the crowd of faces that stand out. Assassins, robbers, crooked security, K-heads and jealous brothers. I catch eye contact, and he heads my way. I repeat my mantra: too smooth to be trapped/too addicted to not come back. My fears fall on the tarmac of the drug-wrapper infested car park.

My reflection becomes trapped in his bulletproof orange Oakley. The incoherent reproduction of the world appears to me as an enticing alternative to reality. He lifts them to get my attention, not display his blood-shot eyes. He grins widely. 'Why didn't you come inside, Aldo span a fucking great set...'

'Sounds like it, I heard the last few songs. But I just got here, these fucking pricks wouldn't let me in.' I pointed out the ex-soldiers hanging around the palace gates, laughing at the state of their ward.

The grating voice went through the usual post-club routine, asking me where I had been, who with, was I carrying. But the mind behind the voice is gone. It's just empty words decorated with colourful but barely decipherable slang

Dee pulls up silently next to us, switching off the ignition of yet another new super bike. He dismisses the tall blonde, turning around to her, 'go and buy a fucking *pancho* or something, just get lost for now.'

Dee stays sat on the bike, although the way he sits make it look like it's the bike that is being sat on. He is what I fear most about Buenos Aires. He is also who I fear most in Buenos Aires. He is a Big Dog, who likes to eat fish just as much as fishermen.

Stay in a city like this long enough and perspective disappears. You can grow so big, so quickly, here that it is easy to lose control, of how to define your own self. I didn't take me long to realise that, in infiltrating the dregs of this city, prejudices are lead weights.

Dee knows about lead weights, concrete too, you'd imagine. Trouble steps down from the black gates of the pink palace, too late, she has already seen me.

I am stranded on a floating island, watching my dreams and good luck sail by. No longer hand-in-hand with the girls my careless sociopathic tendencies let slide through my fingers.

More eye contact, accompanied by complaints of why I am distracted from business. 'This one's going to come over and piss me off,' I tell them. 'Bear with me.'

Flat face and rustic zig-zag hair tightly pulled into a Lara Croft pony tail. She's a Fireblade, fun, but difficult to handle at high speeds. Awesome in experienced hands. Body of an athletic goddess, always a nervous grin tightly stretched across perfect teeth. But pallid, especially at this time of the weekend.

She tucks herself and a cute stranger into my parka. They're innocent, I am not like you, Dee. He looks at me, not responding to telepathy. What can I tell her, can you excuse us a moment, I am trying to cut drug deals with a guy who cuts off fingers when he gets impatient.

I take off the jacket and guide them towards the guy selling *panchos* and sandwiches from the rear of his car. They huddle together and bounce off, a white blob of nylon-covered goose down. The wind cuts straight to my sweat soaked shirt. The layers of fat I need are long gone. I comfort myself with thoughts of tucking myself back into my jacket.

'Are you going to pay me any fucking attention?' Dee snaps his fingers. I start talking business subconsciously, making notes to my black box:

There's nothing I can do now, navigate to a place where they might find my body, where I may last long enough to wash the toxins from my flesh and drive the butter from my lungs. These Big Dogs will finish off the rest and throw their bones back into the river from whence they came. If I was a fighter pilot, I might eject right now, but I'm really more like a relic of some iconoclastic mogul, too clumsy to stay in the air, too new for a museum. I'm even one of those planes dishonourably-discharged special forces guys use to smuggle coke. My pilot's gone. He's bailed with the payload exactly as he'd planned.

Where does that leave me? Will my fast-fading body stand up to the end of this phase of down-and-out tourism? Have I become something else? Is this me or the evil product of my addiction? Is this city the subject for celluloid? Big Dogs on fast bikes, Small Fish dancing and dealing, twenty strong in the club. An underground movement? Or just another drug de-generation? Like my own.

Elevated

Sat at my desk, I wouldn't even bother starting to write. I'd just put my head in my hands. What would I lay bare on the paper, anyway? That I argued with my father over broken Easter presents from years gone by, lost opportunities and destroyed moments. It'd be better to just escape, run through a freshly harrowed field at lightning pace, disturbing the gulls as I flew by. I indulge in freedom and elevation, so much. I can let down my guard, show my person to the world and open the world to my person.

I live on a dirt road. Does this make me poor? Right now the mud is baked hard, but that could change at any one of these moments. This could have been an island the way the weather would change. I'd never be surprised by a crack or thunder or an out-of-place cloud on an otherwise fresh day. You go home wet some days. There's no avoiding these things, not that you'd want to risk missing an adventure. Now I'm stranded on a real island under this mighty tree. It's open ground here and so I feel a twinge of danger. My hair took a good soaking on the way over and now there are potential drops forming in the follicles of my brow.

Soon one will drop and cleanse my eyes. Soon there'll be columns of slightly heavier rain cross this field. But nothing will happen before I make a decision on how I'm going to turn this into a real adventure. These things are unpredictable, and I have to adapt.

I can't remember what we were taking from those little birds. Perhaps we were giving something to them, crumbled old bread. I can't remember if we had good reason for being so passionate, about that or about anything, less a football or my best friend's twelve-year-old son.

There was nothing, no detail, a few words exchanged with my distant next door neighbour. We hurled a few formalities in our loud voices without ever really approaching each other. I'm only going to take a couple of clods of dirt and nothing else. The times we did get up close, he would smile and laugh at how, for so long, I'd taken him for a mean and angry man. One time, he came with us and began to kick the ball around in the dirt field. But he was too stiff to get into it, and when he started smiling and laughing, then things really started to seize up.

I ran some more, onto a set-aside, where the tall seeds of the fountain grass whipped against my leather of my shoes. It was inevitable some of those heads would break off falling in the gap where a tongue should normally be. Perhaps it was only me who had this type of shoes. Perhaps it was possible that no man had ever run this fast. I felt as if I was being elevated, streamlined and thin. Could I take off before I got to that hedge line and the trees that copulated behind it?

That afternoon, I didn't even dream. There was good reason, however, because I don't think I slept either. I lay, watching the light orchestra of creation as it slid across the sky, moved by the blowing wind on the poplar outside my window. The light dimmed and brightened through the shutter slats, as the leafy foliage was pushed in and out of shape. The light waxed and waned as I drifted in and out of reality.

Life's momentum struck me. I was thinking through a series of only not even vaguely related episodes, when something clicked into place. I slapped the mattress. I told myself I'd done something there, at that point. I whooped. I achieved something from nothing, changed the course of things.

It was the first moment of joy, and what followed it opened the path to moments of happiness, feeding back through the entire series of events that had led to a triumph. My head span more as the clouds drifted head long by.

I didn't lay there too long, or I'd never have gotten to sleep. I was drunk when I stood up, a feeling lying in wait for me. And so I lay back down. This time I was on my front. I didn't move. I lay instead, thinking about how since then everything has reversed. A moment of despair passed as I pictured my mother's pain. Life has crossed and double-crossed me, leaving me without any joy. Without the circularity that lifted me, without the speed that elevated my soul, drawing it into linear movements and threatening me with more than just the odd rain cloud.

I haven't yet seen every type of human behaviour. I'm too young and I live on a dirt road. But I can explain a few of them to you. I can be as clear as to use terms of what they look like.

A retired couple sit in a café, side by side. Sometimes they are talking and other times just smiling in peace. In front of them a toddler trips as he mounts the curb from the street, the lady's face drops when she sees and hears the mother reprimand the child. Inside her mind she spirals. When she comes back she retells the story to her husband. He is only mildly interested. She raises her voice as if the volume would impress the significance of the thought, eventually the couple's peace dissolves into argument. The woman shouts as she speaks, laughs and pretends to enjoy the irony, but inside she is dying, and because she is, his life's days also find the promise of abundance no longer harbours the kind of numbers it should.

Pound the Intruder

Pug and I are half way through planning our trip, sprawled on the floor over high-res satellite maps of the Arabian Peninsular. Thinking up crazy justifications for travelling by land during the end months of the summer. We're going to get perma-tans. We'll get so brown it'll never fade. That kind of arrangement. Take the jeep and enter here and cross the way. That's what we would have been doing when I lost my temper with someone ringing the building door bell.

I cut to the balcony. Look down. Two helmeted heads are waiting on a moped. Girls. It is the combination of physiques that stops my attention going back inside the apartment. They are familiar, so I shout down that I am coming down. The faces look up one at a time, Barbie and Swenta, what a nice surprise.

A good few years had passed since I had met them together in SA. We had climbed some tourist landmarks together and hung out, getting into trouble, getting drunk and that kind of thing. They see me and smile. Perhaps they don't seem as excited as me, but I don't notice as I scream at Pug, it's Barbie and Swenta. Bu then why would they? They would have been expecting it to be me.

I run down the stairs, nearly falling in my rush. I get to the ground floor and there's already two neighbours there answering the door. An old woman, one of the three I routinely ignore. The other, I do pay attention to, just in case I don't see him again for nine months. He looks like like the San Telmo professor, bald, sporting a cane and a rigid skull. He asks me how things are going with a mix of paranoia and manipulation.

Once I'm finally allowed access to my visitors, the three of us hug and I notice genuine happiness in Barbie's eyes, and even Swenta looks pleased. We chatter our way up stairs to our landing, where I introduce them to Pug, who immediately brings out their *deutsche* sides. I tell her she can have which ever she wants if she can get them to hang around for a while. I am just glad to see them.

The professor side tracks me on his way up to the attic and speaks to me with his own German accent, undoubtedly questioning me just to practice his English. Trying to get me to open up about my degree and asking me in a way to project my intelligence. Or at least making me put forward whether I am intelligent and out-going or if I followed the system. 'What an interesting subject,' he might have said, 'where did you or are you taking it? What he really wants to ask though is 'what interesting things do I know?' I shut him down with my excitement. This is what I fucking hate about Amsterdam.

We hang out for a few days. Pug tunes in with Barbie. I think. I don't really pay much attention after the initial surprise has died off. The worst obviously waiting to come. Knowing the four of us I am sure we partied non-stop, got dunk and reacquainted ourselves. Surprising how butch Swenta and Barbie have become. But still no signs of flying dragons. Perhaps it is just coincidence, but they also look pretty slick, like they are riding on the fabric. It is possible they are shapeshifters but I am distracted. And no longer by sneaky ways to enter Iran.

Pug comes and meets me on a corner cafe after they've gone. Not as straight forward, your friends, as you thought. I give her the raised eyebrow and invite her to explain over a cup of tea. She paints the picture of the two girls in London. I see it, hanging out around 'The Hook' (The Cut, or any other landmark junction with a stupid and nondescript short name, doing no justice whatsoever). I beg her to go on, making it obvious that I know exactly what it means to be sitting around The Hook slouching all day long on the terraces of cafes writing in note books. Bohemian revolutionaries basically. Perhaps not, she suggests against the obvious. Perhaps even disguised as wannabe writers.

The next thing I know, we've tipped over our table, spill-smashed our half-started, half finished high-tea, and have cut into an alley way. Three or four turns later, with our cardio-vascular systems responding, we find a narrow entrance leading to a courtyard. But it's still wide enough for them to drive a moped through. We run some more, scan every new street desperately for something smaller. 'My lungs won't last at this pace.' No response. She points to an iron grill covering the fire exit to an apartment building. It's either that or a very old dead-end street with a wall and climbing plants. Along the left side of the next street, the buildings lean over each other making the small alley more like a rocky canyon. The noise has gone. Pug and I make our way along cautiously, moving to the right-hand side of the street. We make decisions in time for them to be effective.

We wait, watching the street entrance from which we had just emerged, then started edging slowly backwards. We find a grill and hold it shut, trapping a large piece of discarded card between it and our identities.

A guy falls from the street into the alley; out of breath

too, he stashes himself between two recycling bins. Gun drawn, sucking oxygen for his life. The next man sprints from cover also ducking behind a recycling bin slightly closer to us, someone infinitely more familiar. The moped shoots past us, too occupied with squeezing the line of bins clear of their path to observe us but untouched. The first guy draws out into the alley as they pass, he lifts his gun but points it at the second guy. The moped stops and the rider tries to spin it around, but there's not enough room. This second guy, the follower, I realise I've seen him on some prior occasion.

I misread all the misdirection and draw my pistol. But in the mean time the first guy is challenging the follower. He yells something about being security forces, but it's just bravado. The follower shows him he can see through it, pointing his shifty gaze towards me as we've started to feel like sore thumbs and third legs. The security guy spins around, his arms locked, no slack for recoil. I shake my head and sheath my own gun. Walking over to him. The follower leaves, ignoring the orders to stop.

"Stop yelling. Who is that guy you were threatening to shoot? I live here I demand to know." Pug turns right covering the moped.

The security guy begins to shake and accuse me.

"Let me see your gun."

"It's not real," he confesses, "tell him that he needs to shut up and come out from between the cars."

I take the pair of them back to the main street, making sure my back is still towards Pug, hoping she is not still dominating the moped guy but also watching my back. I check what kind of weapon is being brandishing so wildly in the name of security protection. They accompany me to the daylight and shows me his gun's lack of authenticity. I look at him as if to say, idiot. My lips stretched into a tight disaccord. I glance back over my shoulder to check on Pug. She's way ahead of me, picking the inner door behind the grill, all the while with the guy hostage under her left foot. His arm contorted around her left calf. I tell the fake cop and his friend to be on their way. They wander off having forgotten everything, not even looking like they know which the right direction is.

Having penetrated the building, Pug is already hard at work tying up the moped guy. I come in and shut the door behind me, but before I've even had a chance to look around there's the noise of new arrivals in the street. As I start to fix the security locks, a force tries to push the door back open. It's the follower, the second guy and there's more sounds of arrival behind them. Then there's catch eye contact as we fight over the door's status. I want it shut; the front guy is indifferent so long as he doesn't remain outside. We push and struggle. Without the door positioned correctly, I can't get the bolt to enter. I curse, winning the fight but not being able to secure the door because of its misalignment. "Pug, what the fuck!" She comes and backs me up with her beefy shoulders, watching the door for movements and then placing some well timed kicks to fuck with the follower. I eventually get it shut. The door deforms as I do, the last blow delivered from outside being a hard sharp one. – What just changed I ask Pug, something changed.

I have a preliminary look around the lobby before realising there's a second safety door to the building, on the landing above. My immediate thought is one of size, how many more points of entry. I rush upstairs, Pug catches on and is a few steps behind me. We pull a few plants and ornaments down onto the stairs and pass briskly up to the door. It opens easily and we're soon into an apartment, looking through the rooms until I come to the bedroom, it has double doors leading out on to a balcony. My impatience gets the better of me when I find the door is locked. I finally get it unbolted and step out to see what's going on in the street, thinking I see the security nut outside, I take a half step out and realise it isn't him and that the first guy wasn't alone either. Elaborate and confusing. I struggle with the security lock and then have to battle to get yet another door shut, this one complies more easily. Another guy, maybe even the follower, drops down from the roof on a wire and smashes the entire glass front to the balcony, the inner glass doors smash too and the wooden frames splinter into the apartment, carpeting the parquet in fragments. "Pug, so much for locking ourselves in." We exchange some improvised weapons from the choice of interior design and then get down to the business of pounding the intruder.

The Mercatroid

I was in two minds; one said they didn't deserve electricity, the other that it was a good excuse for me to escape them a while. Two hours had passed since the four of us had installed ourselves in my lodge, my home. When I left to start the generator to the electricity supply, my guests were still talking about the earlier fracas. I placed the wooden door in its closed position and quickly left the building and its four rooms and three occupants.

Emily had been given quite a shock by the stunt in the visitors' centre, although the man's arm had obviously been prosthetic. From our position, the blonde, Charlotte, and I had been able to see the sleight of hand; that's not to say, however, that she didn't jump out of her skin either. It wasn't for that reason that they didn't deserve electricity. Quite the opposite in fact, I needed a luxury or two, you know, to stay poised.

I stood at the end of the carriageway to the lodge, watching the lithe and stony road and its verge of towering evergreen; the orange nebular cloud and setting sun. From below the lanterns that delineate the edge of the road began to illuminate. One by one, starved of the sun's light, they switched to provision, warning late night wanderers and snaking their way up the hill towards me.

My only company was the companions' voices that rattled around the vacuum, my loneliness, resident in my head. The time of the year meant the forest produced no smells and the day no sound.

Clumping back to the lodge I heard a jeep rumbling

down from the pass towards the road. Very rarely do I see people coming down that way, but as my radio and my g.p.s. were in the lodge I nonetheless kept an eye on it whilst heading back indoors. My beacon by the road was lit so whoever it was would know I was close by.

The jeep didn't take the road, pulling up behind me on my way towards the lodge. I stood to one side to let it pass. It didn't. The man in the driver's seat was beaming. He began straight out, briefing me on the plans he and his companion had for the next few days. He had a white groomed beard.

"We've got some of these auto-inflatable rafts with pitched tarps. Figure we can take one out and take advantage of some of your famed rapids in some downhill action. But hey, there's something you could help us with. You must know a good spot for fishing. I mean, we never go anywhere without a coupl'a rods. And it'd be just great to get one of these babies out on a calm lake and do a spot of night fishing, you know? Set up from inside one of these sonobitches. Find some real deep water, we got a couple of sonars." He dragged out the end of the sentence with a grating set of 'r's.

I looked at him for slightly too long and fell into a gaze. He pulled himself from the seat by tugging hard at the roll bar and did so without breaking eye contact. With a spider-like dexterity, he exited the vehicle. I was left no choice than to talk, so great was the fear of being cocooned in the same white silk that grew from the man's jawbone.

"I've got some friends, we're going on a hike. Otherwise I'd love too."

As he got closer I realised who it was, and why he

seemed so familiar. Indeed, the passenger in his jeep was the man with the prosthetic arm.

"Say, you're the park ranger at this here station, ain't that right? You were in the Welcome Lodge earlier. With those pain-in-the-ass city kids. Right? Your colleagues told me I'd find you up here. Anyway… so… look, I don't want to see hide nor hair of that little bitch, no matter how good-looking her friend is… that's right! You thought I hadn't seen you back there, keeping her all to yourself. But I'll let bygones be gone; I'm sure a mountain goat like you ain't interested in all that petty eye-contact status, make-up and *hoi polloi*. You know how you just can't take along people like that, not when you're the kind of guy who likes to lock horns. Like taking a knife to a gun fight, right? So here's what we'll do…" by this time was right on me; so close I could smell a fetid ozena.

"You have your g.p.s. on you?" I shook my head but with the dying daylight it only drew him closer. I attempted to ordain myself. He fought back on the same plane, circling me and ending up on slightly higher ground. He probably only had an inch on me on flat ground, but now he was bearing down on me and I didn't have my g.p.s. so I was also already shaking my head.

"No worries then! Look, you got a pen and paper, I'll give you my callsign and then when you shake off those mukes you hunt us right down. Go on, test yourself, see how close you can get." I shook my head and pulled a pad from the front of my jacket. I offered it to him, he didn't even flinch. I ineptly took a pen from my humeral pocket and got ready to write.

He began spelling and I tried to take down the letters, but I couldn't see well and the pad was loose and felt slightly damp. I looked at him with what must have been a request for pity.

He shook his head, "Try resting on your knee!" and then began again "em, ee, ar, ci, ay, ti, ar, oh," he was following my delineation because I stopped to look up and by the time I had made his eye contact he had long stopped syllabising.

"That's too long for a…"

"It's my name, bobo!" the vocative slid off his tongue and fell toward my lowered position like a corner-first brick.

I looked back to the page and read the letters. Then brought the pen over them to cross through them. Before I had scribbled through the word the man had retrograded, found his haunches and brought his head over my shoulder. "Well, don't cross it out!"

I neck snapped in reaction, the foul smell coming from his nasal cavity hit me again. My head sunk in shame. I told him wait and took a pen light from my pocket and trapped it between my lips, having forgotten that I was wearing a head torch.

"Now, come on. Em, ee, ar, ci, ay…"

"Why are you making me write your name out. Just give me your i.d."

"What's the matter? Are you scared of my name? Can't you even write it. I know you heard it earlier." The pen light began to fade. I switched on the l.e.d. light on my forehead.

Putting the pen and paper into the same hand, I stood up. My ankles had been crossed so I rotated, expecting to find myself face-to-face, but I found myself instead looking at his truck and the man with the prosthetic arm. He was now smiling, exposing a silver tooth. I felt a sharp pain in my back. The man with the white-lined beard had somehow manoeuvred himself behind me again. Another sharp pain. And again. Again and again. He stabbed me until it was dark.

I had been living around that area for 22 years of my 26 years of life. Nothing before had ever happened to stop that. There was just my house, a park ranger's lodge, and surrounding areas of beauty; mountains, forest, countryside, green, chalk and the black of night. Life was my friend, the only one. While I had been away, during those 4 years, I had made some friends. The mind can only imagine the kind of misfit that comes of not growing up with people.

In the reoccurring dream I'd been having, I would be standing on the landing in a luxuriously wide stairway, I've just given up trying to evade a pursuant. He faced me half way through ascending the previous flight of stairs, stealthily climbing. I freeze, suffering. There's a force of air in my lungs, my heart is pumping twelve to the dozen. My thorax is pulling atmosphere in and out my cold lungs via a burning windpipe. I engage my brain in establishing whether if I hit the deck I will be contained within the safety locus of the stairs. Will it make any difference? I can't understand the logic, having never carried a gun myself, but reality's bite feels like a missing body part.

Now I am welcoming friends that I met during those four years I spent studying with the forestry commission, learning what everyone else called the flora and fauna that I had named myself differently. They've come out to practice what they study all year for a few weeks. All their lifetimes' really. The following inter-action however will make my feelings towards their approach blindingly obvious.

The reality of the welcoming them extends to collecting them; that equates to a two-day roundtrip. We crash at their place following a heavy night of catching up and drinking. I wake to find the skin of my face trapped against the carpet by my heavy skull. The bony sphere had slid from the wafer-thin mattress to the beaten and rough rayon carpet. A piece of laminated card stuck to my forehead created a tabletop mountain isolated in hills and valleys created by the carpet's shag. When I sleep on my stomach I nightmare myself awake or fall out of bed; depending, I have learnt to assume, on my sleep pattern cycle. A lottery between rapid eye movement or rapid floor movement.

The four of us chug along in my surviving white Fiat Tipo. The rear window stresses, barely containing the three weeks' worth of hiking gear for three people. We reverse the hangover process with gentle banter and cigarette smoke until we are clear of the rain showers. But no sooner than the windows are lowered, and the smoke cleared, does a difficulty arise.

Emily has always had a problem with me. I could easily figure out from the beginning that it was jealousy; but as time had moved on I think the problem had developed inside her. Of all the people I got on with in a friendly sense, her man, Nathan, was the one I bonded with. So perhaps I am getting confused here with envy, but there had always been a grating sensation in the collective jawbone when we were together. On this occasion she had brought along J; a young almost groupie who was still studying her second year of environmental science. And so far she had done very well in keeping this attractive young arm all to herself. Although more of a sudden equatorial eclipse than a difficulty arising, the coincidence with the smoke clearing from the cockpit of my Fiat meant the appearance of a muntjack on the road was like the blunt knife entering the small of my back. By this time we were travelling by proper mountain roads. It was a fast turn, with camber; and it resulted in my having to swerve. While there was no serious physical damage to any party, there was further upset to the karma in the car. I recover us from the verge and accelerate back along the evergreen corridor. We travel for minutes in silence. I realise my duty to aid everyone back to their comfort zones.

Having said I am a misfit, this provides the perfect case study. What would have been easier for me is to have spent the following twenty minutes replaying the incident. Evaluating such aspects as; analysing the look of the muntjack's face, assessing the sponginess of the brake pads during excessive braking, performing cost/benefit analysis on a discreet piece of fencing against a road-user caution sign. Ensuring non-repetition of the event is straightforward, but what I can't do is resuscitate a socio-human group.

I tell them about the last time I lost control of my jeep. It's an open top with a roll bar, but they already knew this. New information to them was that I only rarely use a buckle because it does turn over frequently and when it does the places I go tend to invade the cockpit; so I've always maintained that it's more healthy to fall out. The exception being when I am travelling at higher speeds, which is only occasionally.

The previous occasion was one of those regular, frustrating accidents. I was on a 55° incline and was pushing the front offside over a large white boulder, gunning the six litre engine with just a few inches to go.

Had the offside wheel made it over the zenith of the boulder, a goal that teased me from just one man-oeuvre away, I would have had an opportunity to rest my arms, as well as the engine.

"I pushed too hard. The last snort of petrol. Perhaps there was some small recess under the back wheel. But I flipped it diagonally over the near side rear wheel, did one rotation, then bailed." I lifted up my shirt and shirt sleeve to show some of the remaining bruises and scabs.

This was what set Emily off. She began rabidly telling the blonde the story of the last time they had been to the woods together on a hike. Nathan had cut himself; a deep but clean slash; so much so that he hadn't no-ticed it. The story was new to me and I found some as-pects difficult to get my head around. Then I had an instance of a reoccurring thought; there is one thing I've never had opportunity to add to my list of dislikes about Emily and that's lying. And looking at the scar on Nathan's thigh in between glances at the road I can see that it had been both very deep and very clean.

What this reoccurring thought does to me however, is make me want to lie. In fact it makes me angry, I want to drag her in by deception. But that's why I have the mountains, to avoid that side, and luckily I could see that we would reach the park entrance office before I needed to do anything.

They were still yapping on about how much blood Nathan had lost and the number of stitches when I dragged them into the visitors' centre. Grabbing the signing in book, I took them in the back office and sat them down while I made some coffee. Four hours driving still beckoned me.

When I came back I found the blonde girl finishing off

her entry and Emily and Nathan gone. The grating voice soon made itself heard, coming from the reception area where she had engaged Mike and two other rangers. The two other rangers did not appear familiar. They were both past middle-aged although one was noticeably more spry. I listened as the two old men patiently nodded their way through yet another recital of the scar story.

As they patiently nodded their way through the story, exchanged the odd glance and changed from one position to another and made full use of the counter, striking various poses like old hands at modelling outdoor apparel. As Emily ran out of breath the more animate of the two began a well-practised, guided corporal tour of the marks life had left on him. His voice was too low for me to discern, what was noticeable however was that he gave the talk without removing a heavy pair of dark glasses. There was something enigmatic about him, I could tell despite him being turned at an angle from where I had become trapped watching.

As the denouement grew closer he elicited raised smiles in both of my friends. His companion, who had been growing more stern and unappreciative with the story and its bravado, suddenly interrupted it. Surprising all but one by making it into a double act. With a sleight of his narrative hand, the silver-haired storyteller grabbed his companion's left arm with both hands, at the wrist and under the shoulder, and wriggled the arm enough to rip it from its socket.

Mile high hijack

What the hell is taking him so long? Cold night has become the only companion since my travelling partner disappeared from this littered and urine drenched street; little did he know of the appalling levels of illumination. The barely overlapping lines of streetlights and sagging black wires have as much consistency as most things in Bolivia. In one of the resulting shadows I wait, guarding the bikes and backpacks, feeling exposed.

He has gone to check the hygiene levels in this hotel here. The entrance, just a few metres down the street, calls my attention one last time before I turn my thoughts elsewhere. Somewhere ten or twelve hours south of here, a similarly frigid air desensitised the noses of Butch and Sundance as they listened to the last lub-dubs of their hearts and misguidedly waited for yet another big score. I know risks are inevitable, being a gringo, but only now do I see the odds of finding comfort less attractive than death in a gunfight.

The lifeless air of the Bolivian Highlands is not always bad, take cycling for example. We hitched way up above 5,700 metres this morning; where we found good roads. With no air resistance, we peaked 80 kph heading down the east face of the range. That's not bad with these fat old tyres. Back below 4,000 metres, however, there is resistance, not so much on the lungs' uptake of oxygen, but on the passage of time. It must be like hitting the bottom of a free dive and realising you haven't prepared for the ascent. One step forward is about as much use as two backwards; perhaps this is what it's like to drown.

A drunk local rolls along the pink, plastered wall like stoned tumble-weed. I can smell the *aguardiente* already. He plays some kind of children's game; roll to the end of the block without head or shoulders leaving the wall. Halfway though each revolution a bottle peaking out the pocket of his dirty trench coat clinks against the wall.

The supposedly defunct street-light above me sizzles with electricity marking the drunk's approach. The noise cuts ground from under my feet. My heart skips a beat. There's no point in contemplating how the drunk will tackle all these obstacles at my feet. I look up. Am I going to have to find a new shadow in which to wait? Am I waiting or really hiding? Did I really hear something? There is no sign of life and the drunk is already upon me. I reach my hand out to guide him on his way.

"*Que le vaya bien!*" he thanks me, and I reply in kind.

No sooner than he has disappeared, a gringo strides into view. He's overly vigilant and looks somewhat entangled amidst his knitted scarf and the strap of his camera bag. This wariness is also obvious in his raised shoulders, his forearms entering his pockets at an obtuse angle. He is top-heavy.

The wasted energy of his over-stretched and drunken gait jiggles the red bobble on his alpaca hat. As he flickers past me, he peers into my shadow and I feel the need to check my watch.

Whilst not being able to stress enough how important it is to me to know which variety of dirt will be sharing my bed, I am also wary of the amount of liability with which I have been left. How could I protect my own gear let alone all his as well? Doesn't he know its gotten dark out here? I'll be mad if the chilling of my extremities and the wiring of my senses are only thanks to his need to haggle over a few *bolivianos*.

I turn my attention back to the gringo in an attempt to replace my worries with the thought of a semi-welcoming place to rest my head for the night. His overborne way of walking reminds me of talk about how not to avoid undue attention.

Halfway through considering why the word 'undue' came to mind, a fuzzy gestalt of life shimmers into my peripheral vision. Coming up the street, the entity precipitates past a duotone wall advertisement like a shoal of piranha touching the sunlit surface of a muddy Amazonian river.

The highland city's piranha are dirty street kids. Anecdotes spring to life as the gang attacks the gringo. At least two pairs of hands clamp each limb. I count at least nine others free to pilfer with both hands. Insatiably they begin to undress him.

I am certain now that he can't know I'm here. The removal of his clothes quietens us both; they drop him on the unkempt floor and his struggle also naturally ceases. Cringing into the shadow, I struggle to feel sorry for him; the intermittent sizzling of electricity from the light bulb above prevents me. All sympathy is blocked by the stubborn orange vision of the light suddenly illuminating.

Sizzle. There it is again. My palms begin to sweat.

Silence returns like a dead man's ashes hitting the crusted street; the group backs away from the gringo. A handful of the swarthier form a rear guard, brandishing dull blades. They eye the naked white man even after he begins to stride away in the other direction. Their movement slows to an eddy. The main contingent of the pack fights and tears though the stolen apparel, slicing fabric along every pocket and zipper.

It may seem obvious, but being threatened with a knife when you're naked must be more intimidating than when you're wearing clothes. My speculation quickly concludes: it's nothing I desire to study. Then it hits me: the more gringos, the more danger. And I was worried about the light above me! What about that bolshie's voice, the one that only I will find familiar, launching into the street boasting about having saved two *bolis*?

I look to the hotel entrance, at the bikes leant against the wall, the four packs on the floor, then back to the shoal of kids. What can I do? Nothing, literally. Only my neck and eyes are responding to thought. As if the air wasn't thin enough, fear has frozen my diaphragm. My heart reaches a suicidal rhythm and just below the base of my spine there is a muscle contracting.

Looking to the stars, I find no new faith, just panic. Will another effervescent crackle attract their attention? Any minute now they'll finish ransacking the gringo's gear. When it goes all quiet again. And what if there's a dry-cooking sizzle of electricity?

I might as well be naked. My neck joins the list of paralysed body parts. Don't come out of the hotel now! I squeeze my eyes shut. Tighter and tighter, but even with my face pointed at the sky and my eyes as puckered as my arsehole, I can still see them, shimmering towards me with their sharpened teeth and blunt knives. Out of my clenched fists cold drips of sweat begin to transpire. A sizzle. I force my throat to swallow. My ears pop. Has the sound stopped? Or is it time that progresses no further? My heart beats, lub-dub. If it can squeeze out one more beat then I'll bring my head back down.

Lub-dub.

I unseal my eyes one at a time. The kids continue along the opposite wall, still tussling with the clothes and camera bag. There are too many variables: the noise, my partner, the light bursting into life. If and when they happen, it'll be my turn.

Lub-dub.

I take a moment to look back up at the light; a red devil flickers inside its refractive glass jail. Trapped. It flashes. I flash. It's over in a flash.

Moving testicles

The first time I woke it was to the warm sensation of a *traba* fucking me in the ass, but more specifically, it was in response to an urge to empty my bowels.

That was the first time my consciousness had emerged for air since blacking out in a back street bar during the previous night. Later, when it broke the surface again, graced this time with greater buoyancy, I lay staring at yet another unfamiliar ceiling. I lay listening to the tick-clacking coming from nearby roofs, extraction fans and air-con units.

The owner of this particular ceiling was nowhere to be seen; neither on the bed nor in the room. I was careful in how I searched the room, the resulting combination of my covert tendencies and having woken with feline alertness.

There was no memory however, not even pieced together with visual exploration. I hoped for a constructive amalgamation and evaluation; but instead, worked my way around an all too familiar flowchart. Is it worth staying for breakfast or is it for the best to get out while the shower is running? Position and state of clothes. Locks. Porters. Cash. Transport. I covet the day that I yearn to make a quick exit and then come back with breakfast.

I looked at the night-stands. Both were littered with evidence that this one-night stand wouldn't love me. Contraceptives and prophylactics from nights long passed, telephone numbers leading to those desperate enough to have defaced the wooden surface with inkless roller-balls and dull pencils. I stopped to listen to the silence again. Where was this person?

I ransacked my memory again hoping for a reconstruction of the bathroom, but couldn't. There was no light coming from under the door, so if anyone was in there, they were in the dark. I slid to the end of the bed, venturing my hands along the edge of the bed and along burgundy sheets. Then lay back again, responding to my vertebrae's weakened state. In listening again, I could still hear nothing.

The city dies on a Sunday. There wasn't even a sound from the street, just those clack-tickings from two stories up. Those who had energy last night are still recovering; those who have it this morning are already on their way to the country. That was all I could hear, the sound of people with nothing better to do, recovering.

I stood up and staggered towards a door I hoped led to the apartment. Supporting myself on the walls, following the strongest source of light in the room, that breaking under the door, I went.

The next room was empty of people. Just the humming of a refrigerator and a blinding brightness. I made my way back, closed the door and fell onto the bed. My bowels gurgled, signalling an uncustomary digestive programme.

Back on my feet I sealed my earlobe against the bathroom door, gently aiming to create a vacuum. There was no sound or indication. Perhaps I was having breakfast bought for me. Half way through doubting that thought, my bowels resurged. Time for detective work was over.

He was in the bathroom. And I had already put myself into a rather indelicate position before noticing that fact. One hand gripped the rim of the bidet, the other the door handle and my left foot trapped a loose floor mat against the back of the door.

On placing my fourth limb I located the missing person. He had been sitting in the bathtub behind the lazily opaque white curtain. As I was placing my right foot against the iron lip of the tub, it slipped on the curtain, throwing it into a flourish. He turned his head but there was only a spilt second of eye contact before it fell back. My bowels then, on cue, performed their end-of-rinse-cycle.

Frozen, I sat watching the diffuse reflection of light coming from his jet-black wig. He remained motionless, having returned to an almost trance like state. That eye-contact had at least reassured me that I wasn't going to pull the curtain back on a post-suicide scenario. I composed myself. But I could only create the horrible prospect of combining my hangover and his renewed joy for life.

I stood up, flushed and began to wash my hands.

– My testicles move on their own, he said from the bathtub. I could see him over my shoulder via the mirror, but had been avoiding looking. I was also still naked.

To my surprise he wasn't looking at me. He was motionless. On his face was a grin he wouldn't use in public. He stared down his naked body. His only apparel the wig, implants and a dirtied white feather boa.

As I turned off the taps and scanned for something to dry my face we momentarily looked eyes once more in the mirror.

— What do you mean? I asked between towel assaults.

— They move on their own. They don't stay still. It's like the body doesn't want them to stay still.

I pulled back the curtain and knelt down beside the

white tub, resting my forearms on the lip. I looked at his face, the same grin, same discomfort, showing his crooked teeth. We had a moment of eye contact before he pointed me to his groin.

It was true. After acknowledging the high standards of grooming I stayed as I was to watching the testes swirl. Soon realising the extent of the hypnotic potential, I snapped out and looked back at his face.

— Sorry, I don't know enough about human biology to explain that. I had to stare him out afterwards. He knitted his eyebrows defensively and let out an alcohol-scented laugh of disbelief. I backed off to reconsider my own problems.

I had a desire to distance myself but instead leant over briefly to examine the phenomenon one more time. The skin churned and eddied, as if subject to an undercurrent, the testes rolled underneath the skin like garden moles; squashing his member gently against the inside of his long thigh before letting it relax again.

— That's not normal, is it? I asked feeling my own intrigue swell. However I was looking less for an explanation than an excuse to stop looking and thinking about them.

— I don't know—, he replied, neither scared nor particularly fascinated by his recent discovery. — What do you think?

I leaned back in closely, looking at him for reassurance. He stretched the loose smile again. Poking and prodding his genitals further didn't let me come to any conclusion. — And you haven't noticed it before? I asked, without any aim of sounding like a medical professional.

He let out another sadness stricken laugh, — I don't know, I bet you think we sit around like this in the bath all the time staring at them, contemplating cutting them off. It's not like that, well, I am not, I am far too accelerated and besides they're as ugly as sin.

— Perhaps you should then. Cut them off I mean. I'd had enough and so stopped fondling his penis, which the blood had finally started to reach. I considered it was a rouse. Perhaps he would love me, after all. It would be ironic. I looked down again and turned on the bath's taps. I lit a few candles, and an incense stick, that were by the edge of the tub. His testicles shrank and ran for cover inside his body as the water splashed around them. I apologised and mixed some more hot water, putting my hand on his shoulder and giving him my own fake smile.

I wanted to kiss him on the forehead, but instead just stood up and walked out of the bathroom. I got dressed and left his apartment. I ate breakfast and worked on forgetting my attraction.

Two men

Two men sat across from each other at an oak table. From above them hung a light that enshrined both them and the table. From above the light hung an air of confrontation.

"Consideration! You'll have to reconsider yourself because I took none whatsoever myself." The man used a foreign language with a heavy accent.

"It's a lengthy process, you know that." The other stretched across the surface of the table. He moved a portable typewriter, the only object on the wooden surface, from in front of other man and then stretched himself on the table again.

"Look, it's my way or the highway. I wouldn't even write this out again if I did want to do it your way.

Loosely in the typewriter lay a demand for voluntary expedition. He pulled the mechanical contraption back in front of him and guarded it with one hand while he typed the date with a monolithic right finger. "Now all you have to do is sign, then we can get under way. Now let's forget this consideration business, shall we?"

"Don't you want something?"

"Like what?"

"Like kickback." The heavy accent said abruptly.

"Well, it will need to be, at the least, a double fee, yours to me, the half that I will not be able to collect, and, well, yes then let's say half of that covers any loss of face here in front of these men," the other man said.

After pausing he continued more spontaneously, "and

then you will have to cover what it will take me to deal with this at home; and as if you were a new customer, and obviously you will have to make the other parties present here today forget what they have seen".

The monolithic fingers, hanging laboriously from his upturned palms, offered the typewriter. His eyes meanwhile were fixed on the subject sat in front of him. They stared each other out.

"Well, there's a chance that these are some of the last words I'll ever speak so there's good reason for them to make something extraordinary. It's only a shame that you don't care, you are the only one in the light. But, but…", he looked into the darkness all around him, the table and the other man. "I know you will all tell this story.

The heavily accented man stood up from his chair and reached for the light shade above.

Using it as a weak spot light he exposed men in suits sat cloistered around the room. They shielded their identities with cuff-pulling forearms.

"Isn't this what you are doing here after all? Lurking in the misery of your fellow-man. Achieving your success by bringing about his failure. My failure! What is it about my failure that brings satisfaction to yourselves?" He sat back down again, this time avoiding the stare coming at him from the other side of the typewriter. He started to sob, eventually looking up and saying, "Jonah, come on! Don't… alright how much will it be?"

Together the other man's cumbersome index finger and thumb violently clipped the piece of paper, whisking it from the typewriter. "You're better off signing. If I have to make you leave this room, or to consult with our colleagues, then you will surely be arrested.

And then no one can help you."

Jonah sat back to dwell on the impact he had caused. He took a short breath before continuing to talk at the heavily accented man who by then trembled with indecision. "It's like rain drops. They accumulate until my mood is bad enough to want to ruin your day, only I live somewhere where it rains all day. Somewhere on the shingle line where nowadays the bottles that wash up no longer have messages in them, where waste from ocean liners gets thrown, you know, driftwood. And in all of you outcasts that I have to hunt down, all I see is the reflection of my misery, the towelling of my dirt."

"You're pessimistic" he replied having broken out of sobbing.

"Look, Dario, the extravagance has finished, it's time to go home. Surely you can't stand being a vagabond any more. That is what you are, you know that don't you?! All this you call luxury doesn't fool me, I only have one luxury and unluckily for you it's time. It's sad for me because all these years I have ahead of me are going to be consumed chasing humps like you, that means I am never going to improve, just find more work-shy ways of collaring youse. Do you realise what an overwhelming freedom that is? I mean compared to what you thought you had.

"You think too much of yourself", Dario spat in reply.

"You think? I think I am a diamond zipper on the coat of some ragged street bum, let's just say it's how I deal with not fitting in."

They returned to silence. Jonah scanned the room. His stony face and avid pupils strained to dilate enough to gauge reactions of shadowy and barely perceptible figures.

Dario stood up again. His action was mirrored this time by Jonah who simultaneously brought a threatening finger into Dario's face.

"Just try that trick with the light again, go on!" The same finger brought Dario back to his seated position. "Come on, you don't want to be here, you want to be back in the bad city. Here you're like some poverty-stricken boxing aficionado listening to the big fight on a boxed-set radio. Put your eyes back in your head and get back in the game. Would you prefer to be in jail here than on the streets in Marseille?"

"Walking through the streets brandishing a sword, come on get your toes realigned with the violent edge of life, get into a taxi, pass the port, and find the grand whore wearing flaming raven hair, purple lipstick and Chanel number 19; crocked up in a concrete stairway, her legs propped on the steel banisters, openly displaying her assets in front of the neighbourhood's illegitimate children."

"You know where you are from and that there you already have enemies; there belies your direction. Stop being a coward, there is no need for either you or them to cut one another down. You can co-exist."

"That's where you're wrong", Dario face turned from calculating to offensive, "you've never taken a life have you. Never to get ahead. Only ever because you've been told. You see that's the difference between you and me." Slavering he accused wildly around the room, "half of youse haven't either!"

"When you've seen a man's intestines flow from his abdomen, when you've bitten deep into the flesh of another man and come out better off. Trust me, then it all changes. How do you think my conscience became to be so stained? Not because of what I have done, but that I have sensed satisfaction as a direct result. You have no idea what it is to cut someone down and then go dancing. You are just trying to suck the dirt life has discarded in the third world back, sinfully back, into your over-burdened reality. Is it so perfect that you need to spoil it? Do you aim to fix some universal imbalance".

Dario grabbed at his right elbow and after a shock of pain subsided he began to massage the flesh.

"What's the matter?" Jonah set the four monolithic fingers of his right hand on the table's edge.

"Nothing, it's just a cramp, my right arm, I used to get it when I drank; like dull pain is the sign of that which dissuades me from furthering myself. It reminds me of a pain I'd get, back when I was a kid, whenever I would read a sharp twinge would shoot through my chest as I lay in bed at night. It culminated one night, but while I was watching a video, I was with my sister watching some classic black and white movie on this old broken video tape player. I overcame the pain that night, but it wasn't a victory more a landmark. I still remember it, even right now, and you know what? Every time I try to press on, the thoughts of the past nag at my ankles like a puppy telling me is not yet strong enough to fend for itself."

Around the room chairs began, one at a time, to scrape. The shadowy figures began to leave, each one making a gruff voiced aside as they left. 'Throw him to the dogs!', 'Piece of cowardly trash' and 'He's just a fucking kid inside'.

Bullet points

The gentleman runs his fingers through his hair only to have it bounce back into position. He has the air of being the boss. His caramel hair waves as it runs the contour of his face; its tips tuck gently over the top of his ears. He switches the telephone receiver from his left to right ear.

"Ok, well somebody sent me a Christmas greetings card with bullet points in it once."

"You are joking of course," the voice from the other end of the line.

"No, dead serious," the boss sounds as if he means it too. In defiance he swivels on his chair, turning back to face the regimental surface of his desk. While his manner finds no way down the telephone line, his voice does all the talking, serious. But from the familiar chatter, we can guess that the voice at the other end of the line already knows about the finely manicured nails and moisturised fingers. Right now, they are busy straightening a pile of papers in an iterative process involving pinching corners. Silent transmission between two close friends. The idea has been transmitted, both know he means it.

"So, who was it then? Someone you work with? It's a bit sick! "

"Some *woman* who works in the station. Never worked with her though, mind. More friends than colleagues, if you catch the drift. Funny though, never figured her as a suck up. "

"She the same grade as you?"

"So they say, can't see how you can compare bloody h-r to real police work though." The boss grunts his point and one of those strong fingers begins to hover from colour to colour above the pages of a day-per-view a-four agenda, maintaining a respectful distance from the spectrum of post-it notes. As if it were a sushi tray, he picks one off and deftly rolls it into a ball using just thumb and finger.

"Fair enough then," the voice replies.

"Humph?"

"You know, if she'd been lower down and all."

"Fucking right my friend." The boss's diaphragmatic grunt this time more of an outburst.

"Sick," the voice replies, accepting the conversation is nearly over.

"Some people just can't get off the job." A pause. "Speaking of the chore that binds us, my boss is on his way."

"Humph! Ironic, ay?"

"We've all got to have one, Mike. We've all got to have one."

"Yup."

"Ok, so nine o'clock then?"

"Yup," is the reply, but it barely enters the speaker's mouthpiece before the earpiece reproduces the sound of plastic matching.

The boss elongates his back, turning the elastic s-bend into a dynamic diagonal, pushing hard against the springy support of his swivel chair. He smiles and composes.

His senior walks in. "Ready for our meeting?" The new figure released.

"Sure, let me just see if I can find someone to take minutes."

Squashed against the yellow doors of the train's rush hour carriage Layla fumbles with her handbag. From inside comes the chirpy sound of an incoming call. She can hear the mobile phone clearly, but not find it. The chime begins to cause the early morning grumblers to stir. The low tones of grumbles accompany the muffled high pitch like kindergarten opera.

"Shut up you ungrateful bastards," Layla swears inside her less cluttered mind. "They all live so far into the fucking green belt, they get seats to go back to sleep on the train.

The tone and pitch of her head's voice–like that of her own, normally over-active mouth and larynx–matches her greasy, peroxide blonde hair and complexion. She hides herself with silence and makeup. "Nice big houses too, I bet. Get another hour's kip on the train, eh? Then cause a shit-stir when I wake them up. What about me, I get up the same time, I bet. Two hours, two bleedin' trains. Have to stay awake on the first one so I don't miss standing up squashed against sweaty metropoles and stoned adolescents on this one."

The train slows into a station. "Hope it wakes the bloody lot of them." Layla still can't find her phone. Curiously and frustrated from the search she lowers her head to the window, only to find it was steamed, scratched and tagged blind. In any case, she is riding to the terminal. The doors steam open, a lipstick and eyeliner leave the over-pressurized environment of the handbag. No longer taking the abuse caused by the ongoing cell search.

"Got-ya, you little twat!" She speaks the last three words, more clearly and slowly enunciated, but still not audible to the train. Yanking the phone triumphantly from the handbag more makeup breaks out. This time spiralling down into the oblivious void between the train and the platform.

"Wanker!" With each word Layla's enunciation improves with equal steps to her demeanour's decline. This time, however, not only vocalised, but the greasy trawl wakes more grumblers. Those already mid-grumble explain the situation to their peers. Standees made various comments and giggles. The kamikaze makeup the only lucky party, however, silent and no longer bound to the muggy atmosphere.

The phone stops ringing, in Layla's face. She sighs through braced teeth, takes a deeper breath and tries to sigh through something else. "Probably just the boss," the voice returns, cowering back inside her head, "'Come in early, if you can, I need minutes to be taken' or something unreasonable and premeditated." She is wrong; a text message follows the beginning of the carriage's silence. Not her boss, the same number that had just been calling. *I nd u 2 dial th@ no. rite now. Said.*

The boss places his well-worn, black, over-polished shoes carefully between shards of glass, brick, metal and carnage. Carnage from its word origin, he contemplates the drift from original meaning. Sick. He acknowledges the delicacy of his path with uncharacteristically dainty footsteps and a steady finger on his bottom lip. The walls around him, the surviving walls, are stained with black and red, soot and blood. The windows have suffered a higher rate of destruction, as well as causing one, but there are still fragments that dangle in place, some of which then fall at undetermined intervals, smashing the otherwise unsettling silence.

He reaches the epicentre. Hard to miss. A black, charred hole in what used to be Saturday afternoon.

Around the innocently smouldered tarmac a handful of stationary figures provide the boss's point of focus. Around them visual panic flourishes, paramedics and victims rush and stumble under tight stage direction.

"What was it then? Car? Bin?" His first words.

"Fucked if we know." The first reply "Could have been a car, but there's no sign of it. We should have got some camera angles from here, and from up there," one of the stationary men points a biro at a distant multi-storey car park.

"Good, let's hope it isn't too far away." The boss loses his visual focus in the slats of the concrete and brick beehive where members of the public overlook the scene. His mind wanders aimlessly before asking. "What else you lot got?"

There is no reply. The boss brings his attention back to his colleagues, not seeming seem to be concerned at their lack of information. He stares alternately at each of them with a lost expression. His brain snaps back to the train of thought he'd been on before stepping out of his unmarked car. He makes a revolution, hands on his hips and begins to speak, pausing before vocalising. "I know why you did this. I understand why you did this." His words didn't seem to be aimed at the stationary men; neither does any respond to them.

"Hmm, what's that?" The boss examines their blank faces after returning from a forty-second daze. "Don't worry, it's a process. Can't you see it though?" He offered a hand to the stage. "How many so far? Twenty-three? You're kidding! It'll be fifty before it gets dark. No, you have to get into the mind of the bomber if you're going to catch him."

The stationary faces stay stationed. The boss walks away, his footsteps on his return heavy and glass-breaking.

Interrogation Room. The future. White walls and school furniture. The boss screaming. "You're a fucking amateur. Amateur. Too easy to catch you were, too easy. Far too easy to catch. Loser." The boss, hands pinned to his hips, leans into the ear of a young man sitting at the table. The man's face is contorted with pain, and he pins his palms to his temples. "You have to do more than two you know," he offers the young man three cigar fingers nice and closely. "You have to do more, three at least. Wanted to be serial. Got to do threeeeee." He re-emphasises the fingers. "No," he says relaxing back to an upright–arms pinned against his hip–stance, "number three is going to damage anyone, except the creator."

The sign on the door reads: PAUSE: Genius at Work.
"I knew the guy was a fucking joker," the boss says proficiently removing the sign from the door. He bends his knees and lays it silently, propped with its face against the wall "Come on, Beslit, knock the door in, let's get this over and done with."
Beslit steps back and sends the door flying from its hinges. As the boss flashes his head quickly to view the inside of the room, he sees a young man kneeling on the floor. The young man is frozen in the middle of some complex home-experiment. A look of hatred in his eyes only countermanded by the comic interruption to his motion. "Talk about red-handed," the boss says systematically bringing his head back into the corridor. He looks at the men around him. "He's really going to need a genius to get him out of this one. Think we might need one too, just to work out all the mess and not get blown up in the process."

"Drop the celly sonny," the boss shouts from around the corridor. "Your days of genius are over," He waves the small crowd of shadows into the room and toward mess of red wires, tubing and terrorist.

"Put your fackin' hands behind your fackin' head," Beslit screams as the end of his weapon closes in on the young man's temple.

"Your turn now, Mickle," issues the boss with a pointy finger, "Give him a good kick, like Betsy did the door."

"Right-o," the next black figure stands his shotgun against the wall, treads carefully over and around wires and tubes and positions himself behind the young man.

The young man only feels the sharp smart of whiplash momentarily before his chin hits his dingy carpet.

Beslit looks up from the floor of the motion-rocked van "Did you have to kick him so hard, Mickle? I don't think he's going to wake up before we get back to the station." The boss leans over from the shotgun seat to defend Mickle.

"Takes more balls to do that than blow up dead innocent people. Even if he did take him from behind. Anyway, we'll do a couple of short cuts until he wakes up. Never know who's going to be hanging around when we get there. Just do something to wake him up."

"Right-o, guvna," Beslit returns to his seat on the bench and stares at the body. Silence follows the faces facing each other from their respective benches. The ten heads nod in harmony with the bumps and pot holes from the tarmac below them. The young man lies on his stomach; a suspiciously short tie binds his ankles, which are pulled up to his backside and in turn tied to his wrists. The man isn't actually unconscious, but he maintains his answers to himself. He thinks, "at the expense of one phone call we would all be dead innocent people. There must be another way."